Safely Connected to Earth

Ethan and his Family Explore the Root Chakra

Created by Yvette Farkas

Illustrated by Jana Rothwell

Cover Illustration and Interior Design:
Jana Rothwell

Editing:
Poh Lin Cheng
Sherri Mellamed
Bella Jasper

ISBN:
Ethan and the Seven Chakras: Safely Connected to Earth (Print book)
978-0-9866551-8-0
Ethan and the Seven Chakras: Safely Connected to Earth (E-book)
978-0-9866551-9-7
Ethan and the Seven Chakras: Safely Connected to Earth (Audiobook)
978-1-7382155-0-8

Published by:
Singing Soul Books
Website www.singingsoulbooks.com
Email info@singingsoulbooks.com

Readers love these books!

"**_I can count on one hand_** the amount of books I've read front to back in a day. These are so beautifully written, I can't wait for more to be released!"

~ Chantel Jameson-Farkas, Canada

"**_Stunningly and beautifully written_**, these are highly insightful books on the seven Chakras! I've heard the term Chakra before, but never connected it to the spine and its direct influence on one's body. I tried the breathing exercise and even began taking notes as I read through the books; there is so much useful information hidden in the stories!

On a personal level, the power of the chakras hit home as I began to make connections to my own life. The follow-up exercises made sense. From my personal experience in teaching children aged 9 to 11 years old, I believe that these books share very important life skills and should be included in school curriculums.

What you have created is very important, and frankly, for people of all ages. These books are fantastic, and I can see being a very important resource added to school libraries, both at the elementary and high school level."

~ Mark Desjardins, Canada

"**_A beautiful, thoughtful, and magical journey_** to exploring chakras. Embarking on a spiritual path feels inspiring, achievable, and understandable after reading these books. This is my type of education – fun and enriching to the soul! Truly a must-read for children, but arguably an essential read for all adults as well."

~ Poh, Canada

"**_I am beyond amazed_** at the talent and genuine beauty and creativity in these books! I learned so much about planting! I will be the first to order many books as this story will be legendary and already is in my world. Thank you and bless your heart for the information that you will pass on to kids and adults. May this help to impact the world in a beautiful way."

~ Mel Kiss, The Dominican Republic

A message from Yvette:

Thank you to all the healers, teachers, mentors, guides, family, and friends who have nourished my spirit and inspired growth. I have so much appreciation and love for you all!

Thank you to my nephews, Ethan and Lukas, who inspired this book series with their thoughtful questions during our many forays into the woods, countless hours in grandma's garden, the cabin, and bee yard, during our early mornings foraging for herbs, time spent lying in the thick, green moss watching the clouds float by and chatting, and of course, reading wonderful, uplifting stories each night after our meditations. It was great fun creating these stories based on many of our family adventures together, conversations, and heartfelt questions about some of life's mysteries.

My dear family, we have created and enjoyed many wonderful memories and moments together; my heart is filled with love, admiration, and gratitude for all we have shared. Thank you for supporting me in so many ways. I am very grateful to each and every one of you: Anyu, Apu, Otti, Attila, Katimama, Chantel, Nicole, Ethan, Lukas, Björn, Hudson, Bennett, Rollo, Gyuri, George, Ernestine, and our family dogs; Zserbo, Lui, Jake, and Moose.

Jutka, Misi, and Robi; I place you in the family category as that is what you are to me. Thank you for your neverending support and excitement about my various projects and adventures over the years. I feel blessed to have grown up with you in my life.

Carla Roter, I've had the pleasure and privilege of benefiting from your wisdom, love, support, and kindness for decades. Your unwavering belief in me and encouragement towards my dreams have meant the world. Through you, I've gained invaluable insights into compassion, witnessing firsthand how it can look when opening oneself to greater love and practicing non-judgment amidst life's challenges and triggers. Your constant support and presence have been a true blessing, profoundly impacting my life for the better. I've grown and learned immensely under your gentle guidance, through our honest conversations, and by observing your own graceful navigation through life's myriad "human moments." Thank you, dearest Kapha Mama.

Marcel; you bring so much joy, laughter, and inspiration to my life. You are one of those rare Souls who has the great capacity to hold a sacred space of incredible strength for me to relax into, supporting and empowering me to be my best and shine my light with the world from that space - a space of deep grounding, respect, care, appreciation, fun, and resilience. I love that you inspire me (and many others) with your own examples of growth and consistently strive for personal greatness. Thank you for being on this journey with me and for gently encouraging me to keep going and do what is important to my heart and Soul. I'm so glad you were "persistent." I feel blessed and excited to co-create this beautiful life with you.

Tom and Lilou, you have enriched my life with your shining Spirits, intelligence, humour, and sense of play. It excites me to see what your next amazing chapter of life will look like, and what beautiful gifts you will continue to bring to the world. Thank you for welcoming me into yours.

Deep appreciation and acknowledgement to all the guides who transmitted key information to be added to these books through dreams, visions, and synchronicities. The intent to have this uplift and empower its readers was obvious. This book series was a beautiful, collaborative co-creation between many that was joyful, easy, and flowed with love, wisdom, and clarity. I am honoured to have been a part of its transmission and excited to share it with humanity.

Jana, working with you in this creative playground has been an absolute pleasure. Your beautiful and clear energy, extensive professional experience, and incredible talent has elevated these books to new levels. What you have created is sheer magic and it excites me to know that many will have the benefit of enjoying your wonderful paintings and illustrations. You have brought many new ideas to the project and assisted in ensuring all the different pieces work synergistically well together. Deep gratitude to you for all that you are and all that you have brought and continue to share with the world. It has been an honour to take this path with you.

Thank you to my incredible writing partner, Wayne Bloemhof. You were the gift the Universe delivered when I made my request for assistance with this Soul project. Your ability to tune in to this vision, feel and deliver its essence, and work in harmony with me (and all our guides) was amazing. It was effortless and fun working with you. I am deeply grateful to you Wayne. You helped give these stories legs on which to stand. You truly are the "unofficial wordsmith for the River of Life," as you often say.

A big thank you to Juliana D'Costa who helped start the process of coming up with and creating the illustrations for these books. The countless hours spent laughing together, working in focused silence, and feeding off of each other's creative and "happy heart" energy was incredibly special. You provided so much positivity, clarity, and guidance that helped move this project forward. I love the frog illustrations - and all the others you did. You are incredibly talented my friend. All the good energy you have put into these books will be felt by its countless readers. What a special gift from you.

Thank you to my incredible user testing group. You read and re-read these books, providing valuable feedback, helping to ensure the information being shared made sense no matter the age or background knowledge of the reader. Your honesty and insight have made these books all the more easily received because you cared enough to dive deep into them, noticing loose ends that needed tying.

Sherri Mellamed      Juliana D'Costa
Poh Lin Cheng   Mark Desjardins
Shiren VanCooten   Maria Kiss
Nikolet Gárdián   Milena Gosevski
Éva Csuka   Carla Roter

Sincere gratitude to my outstanding editors; Poh Lin Cheng, Sherri Mellamed, and Bella Jasper. It was after your edits that I felt good about releasing this work to the world. The time you spent going through these books shows in the quality and final product. Thank you for helping to birth this inspired work with clarity and sincerity.

Hi everyone, I'm Ethan.

My aunt Yvette wrote some pretty awesome books about our family adventures. You'll like them.

My favourite book is the third one; in it, I am a bee who learns about "bee-things" and how to overcome self-doubt. That's something I've had to learn to do in real life too. I bet you can relate.

I'm the main character in these books, but you'll also get to meet my brothers, parents, and other family members. To help you remember who everyone is, I've drawn a picture for you. I like to keep things simple, so I made it a stick figure portrait.

I think kids and adults will all like these books. They feel good to read or have read to you, and you learn a lot of fascinating facts about things like using posture and breathing to help you feel more confident in life.

I hope you enjoy our family books!

Meet our *family!*

Aunt Yvette with Ethan, Lui (dog), Uncle Attila with baby Bennett,
Moose (dog), Aunt Nicole with baby Rollo and Björn, Ethan's Dad (Tom),
Ethan's Mom (Chantel) with Lukas, Grandma Suzan with Hudson,
Grandpa Otto, Jake (dog)

Welcome to Your Journey of Heart and Brain Harmony!

Dear friend, before we dive into the enchanting world of Ethan's story, let's embark on a special mission—one that involves the magic within you!

Take a Deep Breath

Close your eyes, take a big, deep breath in through your nose, feeling your chest expand like a balloon. Now, slowly exhale through your nose. Repeat this a couple of times, and notice how it makes you feel calm and centered.

Heartbeat Connection

Place your hand over your heart. Can you feel its gentle rhythm? As you slowly inhale and exhale, imagine sending love and kindness to your heart. Feel it glow with warmth.

Feel the Vibes

Smile as you imagine something or someone that helps you feel the warm hug of care, the loving touch of compassion, the upliftment of appreciation, and the cozy blanket of gratitude.

* **Care**
* **Compassion**
* **Appreciation**
* **Gratitude**

Let those feelings dance in your heart, creating a warmth that spreads throughout your body. Keep breathing slowly and deeply.

Empowerment Words

As you read this book, carry these potent words with you - "I am loved, I am appreciated, I am valued, I am cherished, I am smart, I am important, I am capable, I am confident, I am worthy, I am enough, and my heart holds incredible power." Whisper them when you need a boost of courage or a dose of self-compassion.

Smile and close your eyes again as you take another deep breath, feeling warm, loving energy permeate your body, soothing and relaxing you completely.

Wishing you an edifying journey filled with discovery and joy.

Crown Chakra
Third Eye Chakra
Throat Chakra
Heart Chakra
Solar Plexus Chakra
Sacral Chakra
Root Chakra

Note to parents and readers:

This is an introduction to the concept of chakras (pronounced "cha" as
in "charge" and "kra."). It shows different ways of interpreting and
approaching situations depending on what lens - or chakra - you are
looking through. It contains many seeds of knowledge hidden "in plain sight"
throughout the stories. When watered, these seeds will empower readers to
intuitively guide themselves towards a deeper understanding and awakening
of their own innate wisdom and potential.

The questions at the end of each section are designed to inspire
meaningful conversation between you, dear readers and listeners.
Use this opportunity to engage in thoughtful, heart-to-heart conversations,
bringing you closer to one another as you make insightful connections.

Root Chakra

Trust + Grounding + Physical Security

This is your foundation. It is your connection to the Earth, your body, and your environment. It's about your ability to survive and feel safe and stable.

Sanskrit name: Muladhara, meaning "root support."

Location: Base of the spine near the tailbone.

Colour: Red

Element: Earth

Focus: To have

Sense: Smell

Bija mantra: LAM

A balanced root chakra:
- Courage and resourcefulness
- Feeling safe and secure
- Being grounded
- Knowing you have enough
  (food, love, shelter, safety)

Signs of imbalance:
- Not feeling safe in your home, school, or life
- Feeling ungrounded
- Feeling fear, anxiety, or self-doubt
- Overindulgence or hoarding (feelings of lack)
- Being insecure, living in survival mode

Affirmations for the root chakra:
- I am safe and secure
- I have everything I need
- I am a powerful creator
- I am in control of my life
- I make good decisions
- I am grounded and supported
- I am loved, perfect, and whole
- I can be or do or have anything

How to balance your root chakra:

- **Earthing:** Walk barefoot on the Earth, and spend time outside in nature.

- **Gardening:** Plant and care for seeds, herbs, trees, and flowers.

- **Meditating:** Good to do next to a big, old tree or high-energy areas in nature.

- **Hug people you love:** Enjoy feeling connected and secure with your parents, siblings, friends, and pets.

- **Deep relaxation:** Lie down or sit in a quiet and natural environment that you find nourishing, soothing, and recharging. Breathe deeply and slowly, and focus on your breath while letting go of tensions in your mind and body.

- **Wear red** clothes.

Safely Connected to Earth:
Ethan and his Family Explore the Root Chakra (Book 2)

Chapter 1: Grandma's Garden

There was no place in the world quite like Grandma Suzan's herb and vegetable garden.

The whole family stayed on grandma and grandpa's farm, out in the countryside, every summer. Ethan and his younger brothers, Lukas and Hudson, always looked forward to it.

Each morning grandma would wake the kids bright and early. They would all go down to that magical herb garden while the dew was still wet on the grass. The garden was so green, so full of interesting growing things, and it smelled wonderful.

Grandma Suzan knew each plant by name. She would often talk to them as if they were her own children. Lukas wore his favourite blue wellington boots this summer, as he didn't like to get his feet muddy.

"Why do you talk to plants if they can't hear you?" he asked, giggling and holding grandma's hand.

"They love it!" replied grandma, "It makes them grow better, and they feel safe and loved."

"Do plants really feel things like fear or happiness?" asked Ethan.

"They certainly can feel scared or happy," laughed grandma.

"They're different from us, of course. They don't understand my exact words, but they can feel my energy, love, and care. They can tell when people are anxious, excited, or sad. Every living thing, even this little tomato plant, feels all kinds of emotions. They can feel afraid, thirsty, hurt, content, excited, happy, loving, or peaceful."

"If you go near a plant thinking about hurting it, it will sense it before you get close and feel anxious and afraid of you. If you send love and appreciation to that same plant, smile, and speak sweetly to it as you walk towards it, that plant will feel your adoration and welcome you with its love. When they feel loved by you, they do their best to grow healthy and strong, so they can share their love and care for you through the nourishment and bounty they grow for you."

"Did you know that the plants you plant and care for consider you their beloved family - even though you aren't a plant?" asked Grandma Suzan.

"Really?" replied Lukas with surprise.

"Really," continued Grandma Suzan, "in fact," she continued, "all plants have a strong bond with the people who love them. They grow special enzymes, vitamins, minerals, and healing essences specifically for that human person. By eating the bounty of that plant's offering, that plant is helping to heal you of any imbalance or disease in your body and mind. This is why it is vitally important to grow at least some of your own food. No other plant will be as healthy and perfect for you as the ones you grow yourself with great care and love."

"Grandma, how do plants know what kinds of vitamins and healing properties they need to grow for their human family?" wondered Ethan, fascinated.

"That's an excellent question, little man," laughed Grandma Suzan. "You will not believe how simple the answer is! Can you guess?"

Ethan and Lukas thought it was the special humus planting soil they added to the base of each plant and mixed into the earth before planting a new little seedling.

"That's a good guess, boys, but it's even simpler than that," smiled Grandma Suzan.

"Have you noticed that your grandpa, Aunt Yvette, and I are always walking around barefoot when we are in the garden? The sweat and oils from the bottom of our feet contain tiny messages about our bodies' health. This tells the plants what we need from them to be strong and healthy. Suppose the message from the sweat and oils tells the plants that something is out of harmony in us, that something is not balanced. They will instantly know what compounds, vitamins, minerals, and other healing essences they need to create to help us heal by eating what they grow for us.

Mother nature is incredibly wise and accurate. She does not make mistakes. What these plants grow for us is maximally beneficial for those who spend time here, walking barefoot and caring for them. No two people are the same, and no two plants are the same. Isn't that incredible? So simple yet effective. Of course, you have to genuinely love and care for your plants. When they feel that you care about them, they care about you too."

"Does that mean that if we grow peppers, like those ones right there," said Ethan as he pointed to part of the garden that had three rows of bright yellow pepper plants, and your neighbours down the road grow the same kind of peppers, that what's inside them isn't the same - even if they look exactly alike?" asked Ethan.

"That's exactly right, Ethan," smiled grandma. "They may even taste the same or very similar, but our neighbours' peppers will not be as healing and nourishing for us as the peppers we grow ourselves. Those peppers were not cared for in the same way as those in our garden. They are different. By the same token, our neighbours' plants will be most delicious and healthy for them."

"Those pepper plants you pointed to are actually your Aunt Yvette's. It's her favourite kind. She prepared the seeds, planted them, and has been caring for them. That means that those peppers will be the best and most beneficial for her. Even if you and I eat them, and they taste good and are healthy for us as well, they will be best suited for your aunt since they grew for her," explained grandma as she knelt down next to one of the yellow pepper plants to gently caress a leaf in appreciation.

"Do you see those rose bushes over there, boys?" asked grandma as she pointed to the Southern part of the garden.

"Yes, what about them?" asked Lukas.

"When your Aunt Yvette is getting ready to make rose syrup, rose tea, rose jam, rose water, and a nice rose scrub, she has a conversation with her rose bushes about two weeks earlier. She honours their sovereign spirit by first asking them permission to use their flowers to make these medicines and foods. If they agree, they both enter into a sacred relationship of working together harmoniously to increase the growth of the flowers. The first thing she does when she leaves her yurt in the morning is to go straight to her rose bushes to thank them for sharing their beauty with her and everyone around us - that includes the people, the animals, and other plants. She gently caresses their petals and leaves and praises them for growing so strong and healthy, for being so beautiful, for sharing their love with us."

"Do you mean she has conversations with the rose bushes, grandma?" asked Lukas incredulously.

"Oh, you should hear her in the mornings! It's a constant chatter of love and admiration. You can tell from her tone of voice, movements, smile, and the energy she radiates that she really loves those rose bushes. You can also tell that they love your aunt because they would do anything to make her happy and do what she has so lovingly asked of them. It is a mutually joyful connection, and do you know what starts to happen within a few days?"

"What?" asked both boys, enthralled, their eyes big, walking towards the rose bushes with renewed awe.

"They begin to grow more flowers. A lot more. Ten times more! So much, in fact, that you can hardly see any of the green leaves. It is truly miraculous to witness a plant respond so powerfully to genuine love and appreciation. It looks like a flaming pink bush with so many flowers!"

"Your aunt then begins to gather the flowers in the early morning when the dew is still wet and the energy in the plants is high. Once she has enough flowers for all the foods and medicines she wants to make, she tells her rose bushes she has all she needs, thanks them, and they instantly stop producing extra flowers. Within a few days, they return to looking like their "normal" selves with beautiful flowers here and there but not ten times as much."

"Wow!" whispered Ethan in awe. That sounded pretty magical to him. He knew that his grandparents and aunt often spoke softly with their plants, the trees, the animals around them, and many other things, some of which he couldn't see, but he had no idea how powerful it could be to focus love and appreciation on something. It made him think about how he spoke with his dog, friends, pet fish, and the plants in his backyard.

Suddenly, it occurred to him that he even had conversations with himself, sometimes in his head and sometimes out loud. He realized that sometimes the way he spoke to himself wasn't very encouraging or nice. "I should speak more lovingly with myself," he thought, the way grandma, grandpa, my parents, and Aunt Yvette speak to me and their plants.

Suddenly, Lukas piped up, "Grandma, is there anything else we can do to help our plants grow extra healthy for us?"

"Yes, there is, Lukas. In fact, I was going to show you boys how to plant seeds based on the idea that we are all one family here to love and support each other's growth."

Grandma Suzan carefully removed a small package from her apron pocket. It was meticulously wrapped in soft fabric. She unwrapped it and showed the contents to Ethan and Lukas. They both leaned in to get a closer look. In her hand, they saw dozens of small, reddish-brown seeds.

"Today is the right time to plant these seeds. We garden according to the lunar phases. Mainly during the waxing or the waning of the moon. There are other important astrological aspects to consider, too, as all the Heavenly bodies have unique energies that can affect your plant's growth and potential. But that's a much longer lesson for another day. Just know that it's important to align the energies of the universe when planning your planting season."

Grandma Suzan walked them to a new section of the garden. There, the boys saw that she had already made three rows of small holes in the soil. She also had three large pails of water that had been warmed by the sun's rays.

"First, I blow a steady stream of warm air onto the seeds to help bond us and familiarize these precious seeds with my energy and essence. Next, I hold them up to the sunlight, letting the rays warm them and imbue them with celestial essence. In the evening, I hold them up to the moon, letting her cooling rays nourish and prepare these little seeds, stirring infinite potential within them. After that, I add a small amount of my saliva onto them, so they can get all the important messages my spirit wants the seeds to know about me. That way, they knew exactly what I needed from them to keep me strong and healthy. Now the seeds are familiar with me and understand me, and they are ready to share their love and medicine with me as long as I care for them too."

"Do you do this with all your seeds, grandma?" asked Lukas.

"Yes, sweetheart, I do this with all my seeds. So do your aunt and grandpa. We each have a section in the garden for those plants which are our favourite and that we grow especially for ourselves. We also have many plants that we share. However, the ones that grow specifically for you are the most potent, powerful, and healing."

"Think of this as a sacred ritual, acting in this way helps to connect everything and everyone together. It's a very special thing to do and is thoroughly grounding, focusing you completely. Your friend Priya might say it is a beautiful Root Chakra way of growing food since this results in both food and a deep feeling of peace and grounding, of knowing your place in the world."

Grandma moved quickly to plant one seed in each hole, row by row. When she was done, she watered each spot.

"I drew this water up from the well yesterday. You need to let water sit for at least a day to clear it energetically and allow any sediment to fall to the bottom. It's also important to allow the water to absorb both sunlight and moonlight, as well as your loving intent."

"Water is a powerful transmitter of feelings, energies, and many other things. We must treat it with respect and use it wisely. It can help cleanse us, stave our thirst, cool us off, and even heal us."

"When you bless your water and send it positive thoughts, it retains the energy of those thoughts and feelings and passes it on to what it touches next. Wouldn't you enjoy drinking water that has the energy of appreciation, kindness, and joy in it? It feels good to drink water that is uplifting, energizing, and loving. Your spirit and the cells of your body enjoy it more. You'll feel good too."

Grandma finished watering the newly planted radish seeds, then she said, "Another reason I wait for the sun to warm up the water before watering newly planted seeds is because cold water would shock them. It wouldn't be good for them, just as you wouldn't like it if I suddenly doused you with a bucket of ice-cold water."

Ethan and Lukas nodded in agreement. They were beginning to understand why their aunt insisted on them writing positive, happy words of encouragement and gratitude onto their water bottles. Their mom, Chantel, did the same - placing power words and positive affirmations throughout the house. At that moment, however, they couldn't quite remember what their Aunt Yvette said was the reason they should chew their water and mix it with saliva before swallowing each mouthful.

"Plants have friends too," pointed out grandma. "They are aware of every other plant, fungi, mineral, insect, and animal around them - both on the ground and underneath. They work together to create a happy community and help each other when necessary."

Grandma's garden had all sorts of plants, flowers, and herbs. There were climbing tomato plants, creeping squash plants, dill, sage, rosemary, chives, peppermint, strawberries, raspberries, mulberries, blueberries, and many other kinds of vegetables and herbs. Sometimes the plants needed to be watered, and sometimes grandma would get the kids to shovel fresh manure into the soil to prepare it for next spring. That was smelly work!

"That reminds me," said grandma as she stopped shovelling for a moment, "There is another way to help plants get to know you so they can grow into powerful medicinal food for you. Can you guess what that is?" she asked mysteriously with a laugh.

After many guesses, neither of which hit the mark, she finally let them in on the secret. "It's manure."

"Manure?!" cried Ethan in utter amazement. "What do you mean?"

"Everything that leaves our body contains important information about our state of health. When we mix our manure into the earth and add a little to the garden, the plants receive a lot of information about us. They will know exactly what you need to feel great, and that's how they will grow."

Ethan couldn't get over what Grandma Suzan had just told him. He looked down at his shovel and realized the connection between himself, the composting toilet in the outhouse, the garden, the plants, and eventually, the food that made its way back to his body.

"Wow, I never thought about it like that!" he said thoughtfully, "It's a full cycle."

"Exactly!" said grandma triumphantly with a happy smile. "Nature has many, many cycles. It's good to get to know as many of them as you can and work in unison with those natural cycles. It will make for a happy and joyful life."

Once the boys finished helping grandma in the garden, they went to explore a shady part of the farm to see what they could discover.

"Look, I found an earthworm!" cried Ethan, delighted, and held the wriggling worm up for his little brother to see.

"Eeew!" screeched Lukas. "Keep that away from me! I don't like slimy things!"

"I'm going to use this one as bait when we go fishing!"

More than anything, Ethan was looking forward to going fishing. Grandpa would be arriving the next day, along with his youngest brother Hudson, who was three years younger than Lukas. All of them were going to hike down to the river for a fishing trip.

But first, there was root work to do. It was time to plant the beans and onions.

Grandma Suzan showed Ethan and Lukas what to do. She had already told them how to energetically prepare and plant seeds the previous day. Today, she was going to talk about their roots and why they are important. She had carefully prepared many little seedlings in a seed tray. Each little plant was about two inches high with 3-4 tiny, soft leaves. Now they were ready to leave the trays and go into the fresh soil of Mother Earth.

"First, we take them out gently, so we don't hurt their roots." She said, showing them how. "Can you guess why their roots are so important?"

Lukas wasn't too sure, but Ethan, of course, knew all about everything.

"Plants use their roots to get food and water from the ground."

"That's right," said grandma, "the roots also keep the plant grounded, so it doesn't fall over or blow away in a storm.

Plants also use their root system to communicate with other plants, fungi, and minerals underground. If one plant is sick and struggling, its plant friends will send healing essences to that plant through their root system to help. There is an amazing communication network underground; plants are talking with each other all the time, sharing information constantly. Isn't that amazing?"

Grandma went on to explain how all living things are connected to the earth. "Every living thing needs food and love. All kinds of foods nourish us, such as the plants you grow in a garden, the sunlight, moonlight, fresh air, the energy of nature, laughter, hugs, and love. You may not think of all of these things as food, but they are. They keep us feeling happy, healthy, nourished, connected, and grounded. Food that grows on the earth is also medicine when eaten mindfully, fresh, in the right combination, at the right times, and in the right amounts.

There is an art to growing, preparing, eating, and even digesting food. Food eaten for nourishment is connected with the Root Chakra."

"Plants grow up, up, up towards the sunlight. Their roots grow down, down, down, deep into the earth, connecting with her soothing, grounding energies. The root energy of our world is a living miracle. It is very healing and the reason why it's so important for people to walk on the grass and the soil barefoot as often as possible. This special, grounding energy is deeply soothing for our nervous system, it calms us down, and helps keep us feeling good."

"Every plant, tree, weed, and blade of grass is like a tiny, unique piece of love, coaxed out of the soil by the warm sun. Look how wonderful our little seedlings are. They are bursting with life - so happy and excited to shine their spirit through their leaves, flowers, fruit, and seeds."

"Some plants like to grow together, like tomatoes and onions. Other plants don't want to be too close to each other. A good gardener pays attention and knows just where each plant likes to grow. They will know which ones are best friends and which ones prefer to stay apart."

"Beans like to climb up high," holding onto things with their curling tendrils as they grow. Grandma Suzan showed them how to plant the beans up against a frame of sticks and the fence.

The three of them dug into the ground, planted the beans, and then carefully patted the soil down, so the little plants were steady and safe. Next, they gently watered each spot with the well water that had been infused by the sun and moon and their happy thoughts.

Grandma Suzan reminded Ethan about what they had learned about the first chakra from Priya and her mother. (They were Ethan's neighbours from the first book, as you may remember).

Ethan explained to Lukas how the chakras are like pools of energy in our bodies. Although we have many chakras, there are seven main ones to understand first. The Root chakra is the first one at the bottom of your spine.

"Every chakra has its own energy, colour, sound, vibration, purpose, and its own lessons." Said Ethan.

The first chakra is red, and it is full of strong earth energy – the force of life itself.

The lessons from the first chakra are about feeling safe and grounded, of getting enough food, and feeling good about our home and earth. It's also about overcoming the things we are afraid of.

When our root chakra is healthy, open, and strong, energy flows smoothly, like a river. We feel good about life. We're steady on our feet. We are connected and grounded.

When it is unhealthy, it dams up like a pond, and then we might get sick, feel tired, or easily get scared.

"I'm not afraid of anything!" said Lukas.

"Oh really? Is that so…" Grandma Suzan smiled and winked mischievously at Ethan.

"Let's go into the kitchen and see if anyone has started breakfast yet."

Root Chakra Discussion Questions

1. How do you feel about plants, herbs, trees, and all green and growing things around us? Do you have a favourite type of tree or flower? Why is it your favourite?

2. Do you like to get soil and earth on your hands? What about your feet? Do you enjoy walking barefoot on grass, earth, or sand? How does that feel to you?

3. Have you ever felt sad, frustrated, or empty when you've spent too much time indoors? Have you noticed how your energy improves when you go outside and spend time near trees, walk barefoot in the grass, enjoy the warm sun shining on you, and get some exercise?

4. Do you feel as if you are a part of nature? Or do you feel separate from it? Why do you feel that way?

5. Do you ever talk to plants and trees? If it makes you feel good when someone says you are special, strong, beautiful, and loved, do you think a tree or plant would feel good if you said the same things to it?

6. Ask your parents these same questions.

Chapter 3: Who's Afraid of Spiders?

It wasn't long after breakfast before Lukas had to swallow his words. As it turned out, quite a few things scared him.

Ethan climbed the stairs to the attic where their bedroom was and found Lukas standing on top of a bed, holding a shoe, and completely still with his eyes open wide.

"What's wrong?" asked Ethan.

"Spider! A big, evil spider! Over there. Don't come too close; it will jump on you!"

Ethan tried hard not to laugh, but he couldn't help himself. However, when he went to look at the spot where Lukas was pointing, he got a big fright too.

There, on the ground, peeping at them through far too many eyes, was the biggest, meanest spider he had ever seen. It ran under the bed where Lukas was.

Lukas yelped and jumped across to the next bed. "Get it away from me!" he screeched.

Their dad came into the room to see what all the commotion was about. They both pointed to the spider hiding under the bed.

"Well! Isn't he a beauty," said their dad, bending down to look, "It's a Giant House Spider. Don't worry kids; he's harmless."

Ethan and Lukas were not convinced. Dad had to trap it in a container and take it out of the house before they would come down from their beds.

Grandma Suzan stood in the doorway, chuckling.

"I think both your root chakras need a little bit of work. When your Aunt Yvette arrives tomorrow, she will know how to help the two of you."

For the rest of the day, Ethan and Lukas stayed busy on the farm, but when it got dark, Lukas started to get anxious again. He wanted more lights on in the attic. He checked under the beds several times, and in all the cupboards before he finally got into his bed. No spiders anywhere. Or so he hoped.

But then the power went out, and it was so dark! Even though their eyes were open, they couldn't see anything, not even the faintest sliver of light. Back home, they had night lights in their rooms, and there was always a little light from their computers or the hallway. But not now. They couldn't see a thing.

It was a long time before the two boys finally fell asleep. All night Lukas had dreams about worms, spiders, and nature's creatures. At first, he felt afraid of them, but then, he saw how they weren't bothering him, they were simply going about their everyday bug lives. After that, he relaxed into a deep and peaceful sleep.

Chapter 4: The Family Roots

All the next day, Ethan and Lukas waited for grandpa to arrive. It was early afternoon when they finally heard the truck's horn from a mile down the farm road. The two brothers raced each other down to meet them.

Halfway down the drive, grandpa stopped the truck, while the boys jumped up into the back, and then they drove up to the house together. Aunt Yvette sat up front. Hudson, who was three years younger than his brother Lukas, was there too, visiting for the weekend. Next to Hudson was his friend, who happened to be invisible.

Ethan and Lukas knew all about things like that. They were used to imaginary friends.

"What's his name?" asked Lukas, and then teased, "Or is it a girl?" Ethan giggled.

"Of course, it's not a girl! His name is Kolakesh," said little Hudson. "He has feathers, a green hat, and a trunk like an elephant. He says hello, and he also says that he likes it here because everyone has good vibes."

It was a happy meeting. Everyone was glad to see each other and excited to spend some time on the farm and in the surrounding forests (and let's not forget about invisible Kolakesh, who was most welcome too).

"Well, you latecomers have missed lunch," said grandma, "but I saved some food for you if you're hungry. Kids, help your aunt take her things up to her tent. I mean - your aunt's yurt."

Aunt Yvette lived in a weird home. It was a big, white and blue, round tent called a yurt. She told them that it was the kind of home first used by nomads centuries ago. It had a large, round, cozy room inside with many of Aunt Yvette's things from the far-off countries she had visited. None of the boys had seen such a home before.

"Kolakesh wants to know what a nomad is," said Hudson.

Aunt Yvette smiled at Hudson, then looked to his right where Kolakesh was standing, and said, "That's a very good question, Kolakesh."

"A nomad is a person who doesn't keep his or her home in just one place. Nomads move around to different places according to the seasons, food sources, tribe gatherings, and other reasons.

For example, the Huns (now known as Hungarians), Mongolians, and many other peoples often lived in yurts and moved according to where the animals migrated to in the spring or fall. They knew how to live in harmony with nature and understood how to read the cycles of mother nature. Most ancient cultures had this knowledge and used it wisely."

"What do you mean by 'the cycles of mother nature'," asked Lukas as he bent down to pick up an acorn that had fallen in between some leaves.

"That acorn you picked up, Lukas, represents one part of the cycle of mother nature, sometimes also called the cycle of life," began Aunt Yvette.

"That acorn is a seed. It contains all the information of its life cycle within it. If you plant it in favourable conditions, it will begin to grow, and when it's big enough, it will grow more acorns which will then fall to the ground. Some are eaten by the many woodland animals of the forest, while others bury deeper into the ground to begin the cycle of life again by growing up to become acorn trees. Many of the leaves and acorns that fall to the ground each autumn add important nutrients to the soil which feeds Mother Earth. This makes a full cycle. Every beginning has an end, and each ending has a beginning."

"It's hard to imagine this little acorn growing up into such a big tree, but I guess people do the same thing, we grow from little babies to big adults. Somehow, our bodies know what to do," remarked Lukas as he turned the acorn over in his hand to look at it more closely.

"You are right Lukas," smiled Aunt Yvette, "this information is encoded in our bodies and energy signatures. What's even more remarkable is that this information, or codes of light, can be turned on, off, or even changed with the power of our beliefs and emotions. But that's a story for another day," laughed Aunt Yvette as they continued their walk.

"For now, let's finish our talk about the cycles of nature, what do you boys say?" Asked Aunt Yvette.

"Kolakesh agrees," piped up Hudson, as he held up a leaf to the sun and watched how the streaks of light made a bright orange halo around it.

"Every living being can tune in to these cycles and all the information it contains. These include the knowledge of the star systems, the lunar cycle, solar flares, the cycles of the seasons, the cycles of Mother Earth, and the natural cycles of the trees, plants, animals, bugs, and even humans. Our physical bodies, minds, and energy bodies all have natural rhythms."

Ethan looked up at Aunt Yvette with a quizzical expression, "How do we know we are living in harmony with these rhythms? What happens if we are out of tune with these cycles?"

Aunt Yvette smiled as she closed her eyes for a moment to ponder Ethan's question as she took a deep, slow breath, inhaling the fresh scent of pine needles. It was one of her favourite forest scents and made her feel instantly relaxed and content.

"Another excellent question. You boys are good at knowing what to ask," she mused.

"Yes, even we humans have natural cycles. When we live in harmony with nature and her rhythms, we live in accordance with the natural laws of the universe. You know you are living in harmony with the universe when things flow easily in your life. When you live against the natural harmony or rhythms of the universe, problems begin to arise, sickness begins to develop, crops begin to fail, and the natural patterns of the world - both inner and outer - begin to show a disturbance. Thankfully, there is a lot we can do to reverse this, but it requires a humble approach to living with mother nature. This means we do not try to control or go against her wisdom, but rather, learn from her and work with her natural rhythms and cycles. This is best for all involved."

Hudson suddenly piped up, "How did nomadic people, who moved around a lot, take their homes with them?"

"Nomadic people built flexible, easy-to-assemble homes called yurts in English. This made it easy for them to move their homes. Mongolians call these homes a 'Ger'. Hungarians call them 'Jurta'. A family can build a yurt in a few hours and take it apart in a few hours. When nomadic people are ready to move, they easily disassemble and take their homes with them. "Have you boys ever seen a round home?" asked Aunt Yvette.

"No." They responded wide-eyed.

"Why are yurts round?" asked Ethan inquisitively.

"There are several reasons," responded Aunt Yvette thoughtfully.

"First and foremost, from a spiritual perspective, a circular shape is considered sacred. It represents the divine all around and within us. It is part of the sacred geometry we find in nature. One becomes two and then two becomes many - just like the Vesica Piscis, Tree of Life, and Flower of Life symbols. The "one" holds all the original information. Having sacred geometry in your environment helps to keep your vibrations high, positive, and in tune. It helps keep you grounded, healthy, and clear-minded. It reminds us of our connection to the divine - to our Source - and increases our mental, physical, and energetic resilience."

"Living in a round space is soothing for the Soul. It is also symbolic of the concept of impermanence, which means that nothing stays the same forever."

"Living in a yurt reminds us to be flexible like the wind moving around the trees, mountains, or the river that gently flows around rocks, logs, and other objects in its way. It doesn't fight obstacles; it becomes flexible and moves around in the places of least resistance. Living in a round space reminds us to be open and gentle with what life offers."

"Isn't it too cold to stay in a yurt in the winter?" wondered Lukas.

"Another excellent question, Lukas," replied Aunt Yvette, "One of the reasons living in a round home such as a yurt is practical is because of the magical way air flows inside of it."

"You only need a small wood-burning stove with minimal wood to heat the entire yurt. Heating a circular space is very energy efficient even though there is a large hole at the top of the yurt from where you can see the sky and the stars at night if it's open. The heat inside a yurt circulates around, keeping the entire space nice and warm. Unlike a square or rectangular home where the warm air rises to the top, the warm air in a yurt circulates around and around. Even when someone opens the door to enter or exit a yurt and it's cold outside with icy wind, it stays warm inside."

"There is lots of fresh air, yet it is warm inside. It's the best of both worlds. In the summer, when it gets really hot outside, you don't need air conditioners because the unique round shape of the yurt keeps the air cool. The best thing of all is that you get to enjoy being close to nature when you are in your yurt - you can hear the wind rustling the leaves in the trees, you can see the moon and the stars at night from the hole in the top of the yurt, you can hear frogs croaking, and crickets chirping. It's very beautiful and peaceful living in a yurt. You feel in harmony with mother nature. I love living in my yurt!"

"You said yurts are for people who move a lot. Are you going to move, Aunt Yvette?" asked Lukas, looking worried.

"Not for a long while," laughed Aunt Yvette, "so don't you worry, I plan to be here all year. Grandma tells me that you two boys had a run-in with a big spider last night. Were you scared?"

"Not really," said Lukas, pretending to be brave as a lion. Out of the corner of his eye, he saw that Ethan wanted to say something, but Lukas pinched his arm.

"Ow! What did you do that for?"

"Where is the spider now?" asked Hudson. "I like spiders. I wish I could have seen it." "Well, not to worry, there are plenty more around here. I'm sure you'll see them soon." Lukas didn't like the sound of that. "More spiders? One was more than enough!"

"I tell you what," said Aunt Yvette, "why don't the four of us – I mean the five of us, including Kolakesh – go up the hill and practice grounding our root chakra? That will help us to muster the courage to face our fears."

Root Chakra Discussion Questions

1. Is there anything that frightens you?

2. Ask your parents if they are ever afraid of anything.

3. What does it feel like to be scared? Where in your body do you feel anxiety?

4. How do you act when you are afraid? Do you want to change this?

5. What makes you feel better when you are scared?

6. Do you feel relaxed and safe at home and with your family? Is there anything at home that makes you feel nervous?

7. What's it like to have a home and a nice bed in which to sleep? Can you imagine a life without a home or bed? What do you think that would be like?

8. Do you think that nature is your friend? Does anything about nature frighten you?

9. Can you think of anything that is permanent - that doesn't change? Or do you think that most things are impermanent (they change)?

10. What things in nature have a spherical (round) form? Can you name at least 5?

11. Would you enjoy living in a yurt? Why?

12. Would you like to have your own garden to grow fruits and vegetables in when you are older? What would you like to grow?

13. Do you help out with chores at home? What do you think you could help your parents with? Is there anything you would like your parents to help you with?

14. Ask your parents these same questions.

Chapter 5: Grounding

The three boys, along with Aunt Yvette and Kolakesh, walked up the hill
behind the farm. Near the top was a big oak tree that had stood there for
many years. Around it was a patch of fresh green grass.

"This is the perfect spot," said Aunt Yvette. "Why don't we all take our shoes off?"

"Kolakesh doesn't wear shoes," Hudson said.

"Lukas doesn't take his boots off for anything," said Ethan, but after a little
bit of convincing, Lukas finally kicked off his blue Wellingtons.

"The grass tickles my feet," he giggled, wiggling his toes.

"Ethan, your parents told me about your new friend, Priya, and the lessons
you learned about the chakras. Tell us about them."

Ethan explained about the chakras again. (Can you remember where the
seven chakras are found and which colours go with each one?)

When he was finished explaining, Aunt Yvette reminded everyone that the
lesson from the first chakra had to do with facing our fears, feeling safe, and
learning to trust.

"We need strong roots, just like this majestic, old tree, so we can stand tall and have courage. Let's say hello to this beautiful oak tree and ask if we may share the space with it. Perhaps our friend (the Oak) will help us learn how to ground ourselves. Let's go over and get acquainted, say a loving hello, and stand close to it."

"Trees have life energy, too, just like us." Aunt Yvette said. "We can connect with trees and ground our root chakra with the earth at the same time."

How to be a Tree

"How do we do that?" asked Hudson with a quizzical expression while he looked high up to see the uppermost branches swaying in the wind.

Without meaning to, he began swaying his body in time with the branches while looking up. The others were watching him quietly, waiting for him to 'come back to earth'. They all knew that Hudson liked to get lost in the moment when he was outside in nature.

Finally, Hudson looked back down toward everyone and laughed when he saw they were all smiling and waiting for him.

"To answer your question," began Aunt Yvette, "we first make sure our hearts are open as we lovingly greet the beautiful tree we have chosen. Listen to your inner voice and feelings to guide you. Acknowledge and be respectful towards all of life. They can feel your thoughts and emotions, so they will instantly know if you are approaching them with loving or hurtful thoughts. Mother nature has many wise secrets to share if you know how to listen with your heart."

"Next, stand with your bare feet on the grass beside your chosen tree. Your toes should point straight ahead, and your feet should be a few inches apart, in line with your shoulders, more or less."

"Like this?" asked Lukas as he stepped closer to the beautiful great oak, pointing his bare feet towards its trunk. "Is this close enough?" he asked.

"Yes, Lukas, that's perfect," replied Aunt Yvette.

"Boys, let's take Lukas' lead and stand around this magnificent oak tree together."

The five of them stood facing the oak tree about two feet away from its trunk, sending love and gratitude to it.

"Hang your arms down, spread your fingers out, and let your whole body hang nice and loose yet straight like a tall tree. Let the bottom half of your body become heavy as you imagine it sinking into the ground. Feel all your weight sinking down, down, down to your toes and into the earth. Relax your knees and your hips, and keep everything nice and loose while taking three deep breaths."

The boys and Kolakesh all had their eyes closed as they took a deep, slow breath, then another, and another.

"Place the tip of your tongue on the roof of your mouth to create a complete energy circuit. Feel the soles of your bare feet touching the ground. How does it feel? Can you feel a tingle? Is it warm or cold?

Pay attention and connect with that earthy feeling.

Aunt Yvette could sense the boys and Kolakesh had tuned in to one another, Mother Earth, and the great oak tree as they were breathing gently in unison.

"Gently cup your toes and imagine pulling wonderful, nourishing energy up from Mother Earth through your feet, up your legs, and expanding through-out your body."

"Now sway like a tree gently in the breeze as Hudson did earlier. Is your tongue still on the roof of your mouth? It should be," smiled Aunt Yvette.

"Imagine energetic roots growing from your legs down into the ground beneath you reaching the core of the Earth. Feel how your feet are connecting to your beloved planet. Grip the ground with your toes by cupping the earth. Feel how they are grounded and solid. Nothing can push you over, not even a big storm."

"See in your mind how the trees dance when the wind blows. Imagine how it feels to have wind flowing all around you and through your branches. Imagine the warmth of the sun shining down on you and how good that feels. Imagine cheerful birds chirping and having happy conversations in your branches as you gently sway. Imagine the nutrients and water coming up from Mother Earth through your roots, into your trunk, then up to your branches feeding every part of you - even your tough bark and soft leaves."

"Imagine how the butterflies tickle you as they fly around your leaves in delight. Imagine feeling safe, happy, loved, and deeply connected to all of life all around you."

"Feel the air all around you, and sway this way, and that way, keeping your feet planted, dancing slowly and gracefully, just like a tree in the breeze. Play with the wind. Have fun together! You can spread your arms out like branches."

"Take three deep, slow breaths and smile gently."

"How does that swaying feel as you breathe? Did you know that trees breathe too? When trees breathe, they clean the air for us."

"When you breathe in, imagine warm, tingly energy moving all through your body. When you breathe out, imagine that you are creating a clean, pure, and strong shield of warm light around yourself."

The boys and Kolakesh were all swaying their bodies in time with the wind, their breathing, and the great oak's branches. They felt at peace, connected, and completely grounded.

"Know that you are safe and loved. You are smart and strong enough to handle anything that comes your way. You are confident and wise. You are perfect, important, and capable."

"Kolakesh wants to know how being scared can help us," said Hudson quietly as he gently opened his eyes.

"It's normal to feel scared sometimes," responded Aunt Yvette.

"It can be a good thing in small doses because it makes you pay attention to what's happening right now, right in front of you, and that can help keep you safe. Fear teaches us to be smart and careful, but there's no need to be afraid all the time. Usually, that kind of fear is only our imagination."

"This feels so good," murmured Lukas as he continued to sway his body. "I like feeling grounded and relaxed like our tree friends."

They all nodded in agreement as they continued to stand tall and straight, gently swaying with the natural rhythm of the universe that all sentient beings can tune in to and feel.

"And that, kids, is what it feels like to be grounded, strong and powerful, yet flexible, light, and free," remarked Aunt Yvette as she stepped up to the great oak to give it a big hug. Suddenly, everyone else did the same, and the five of them stood in a circle around its trunk with their arms wide, sending love and appreciation.

Root Chakra Discussion Questions

1. Do you feel connected to the earth? Do you feel "grounded?" What does that feel like to you?

2. Can you imagine what it feels like to be a tree? How would you describe that to someone?

3. What do you see when you imagine roots growing out under your feet, connecting you with Mother Earth? Do you see colours or shapes, or feel or hear something?

4. Why is it important to let people finish a thought or an experience they are having without interrupting them when they are "deep in the moment?"

5. Can you patiently wait and "keep space" for others when they are speaking or in deep thought, or do you regularly interrupt people? If you interrupt, why do you do that? How does it feel when people interrupt you?

6. How can you kindly let people know when you need a break, or some time for yourself?

7. How do you recharge and ground yourself when feeling anxious or scatterbrained?

8. When you think of home, what comes to your mind? What makes your home feel like a safe place?

9. How do you feel after spending time with family or friends? How can they help you feel more grounded and secure?

10. Have you ever tried doing something like yoga or meditation? How did it make you feel?

11. What do you like to do when you need to relax and calm down?

12. Can you think of a time when you helped someone else feel safe and secure? What did you do? How did that make you feel?

13. Why do you think it's important to listen to your body and take care of your physical needs?

14. Ask your parents these same questions.

Chapter 6: Fishing with Grandpa

Early the next morning, grandpa took the three boys and Kolakesh down to the river. It was quite a long walk of over five kilometers, so they had plenty of time to chat.

"Are you afraid of anything, grandpa?" asked Ethan.

Grandpa laughed. "Yes," he chuckled, "every time your grandma gets on the snowmobile, my heart suddenly starts to beat faster! I'm just kidding. She is actually a really good fixer. She has managed to build and fix a lot of the buildings and items you see around the farmhouse. Everyone on a farm must have a good variety of skills to fix things when they break down, or be creative and make something from scratch."

"No, grandpa, I mean, are you afraid of spiders and snakes and monsters?" asked Ethan again.

Grandpa scratched his beard, thinking, as they trudged along the forest path. After a moment, he said:

"You know, the only real monsters are the ones in our imagination. Plants and animals are never mean or evil. Most of them will never harm us unless we act careless or disrespectful. They belong here on earth with us. Some animals, like wildcats and coyotes, might think that we're their food, and other animals, like venomous snakes, are dangerous. But none of them are evil."

"So you're never scared?" asked Lukas.

"Animals and bugs often get scared of us, and then they try to protect themselves. Sometimes all you have to do is to tell them that you're a friend. You've got to open your heart and connect energetically with love and peace so they can feel your intentions and understand that you don't mean to harm them."

"Nature - including animals, bugs, and plants, can all sense your energy, so it's important to be mindful of how you feel and the vibration you are emitting. Do you remember how your Aunt Yvette always does a short meditation with you boys to create a very loving, respectful, and happy energy before she takes you out to her beehives? That's because if you feel loving, kind, and good, the bees - and all of nature - will feel that, and there is less chance of them getting scared of you."

"Depending on the situation, you may even be able to talk out loud with a calm, reassuring voice or mentally with your thoughts and treat that animal or insect with respect. Give them space, and they will probably go away by themselves. They have lives of their own, you know. They aren't too interested in us. However, if possible, you should leave them alone, and you be the one to move out of the way."

"Now, having said all of that, you also have to keep in mind that animals who live in nature are not very trusting of humans. They follow their instincts, so if you happen to come across their territory, they may think you are trying to attack them and feel scared. You have to be careful because while sending out loving energy is good, you also have to realize that a scared animal can be dangerous if it thinks it needs to protect itself from you. In that case, you need to carefully retreat and leave them alone."

"Are there dangerous animals here in the forest?" asked Lukas, who was walking up ahead but still listening.

"Be careful about turning over rocks and tree stumps in the woods – sometimes you'll find a rattlesnake underneath. Other than that – we've never had any trouble. No wildcats here. We see foxes that we have to keep away from the chickens and brown bears that we keep away from the bee yard."

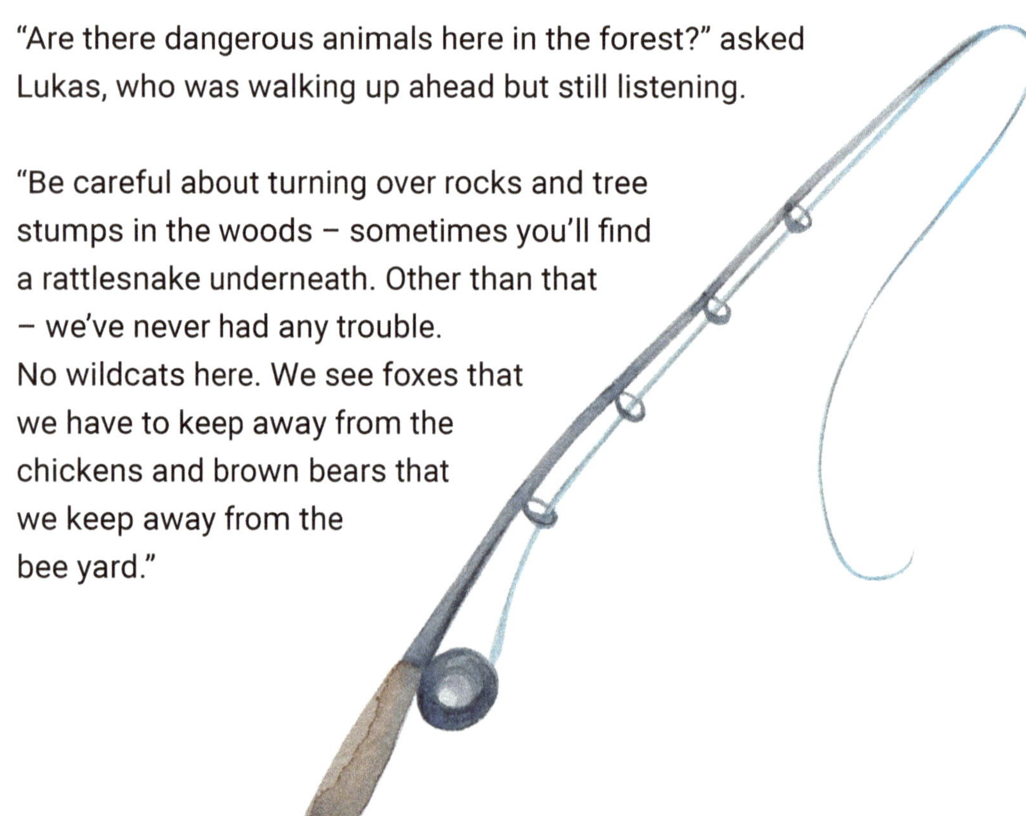

"Aunt Yvette says fear is often our imagination getting the better of us,"
said Ethan.

"She's right," agreed grandpa, "like when the lights go out, and it's pitch dark
– we imagine all kinds of things there in the dark – but when the light comes
on again, there's nothing there. We just make ourselves afraid for no reason,
mostly. In a way, all fears are like that. When we face those fears, they
dissolve in front of us as we realize it really was just our imagination."

Hudson had the shortest legs, and he was getting tired, so grandpa lifted
him up on his shoulders and carried him the last stretch down to the river.
Ethan and Lukas carried the fishing rods and bait.

Root Chakra Discussion Questions

1. When an animal doesn't feel safe, it does whatever it thinks is necessary to protect its life or the lives of its family. This is a Root Chakra response. Can you think of situations where people may feel the same way?

2. Do you think people have instincts - strong emotional and instant reactions - like animals - that bypass thoughts and go directly to a deep emotional feeling and response?

3. How can people calm themselves down and think more clearly even when feeling strong emotions such as fear or anger?

4. What do you do to calm yourself down or change how you feel when scared?

5. What are some ways you can create a safe and peaceful space for yourself at home or school when you need to rest or calm down?

6. How do your friends calm down when upset or anxious? Do they do the same things you do to relax?

7. What do you think makes a place feel safe or unsafe? How do you know when a place feels just right for you?

8. Have you ever seen animals in their natural habitat? Which ones?

9. What do you think animals do to keep themselves safe in the wild?

10. Do you have any pets? What do you think their life would be like in the wild?

11. Why do you think it's important for animals and people to feel safe?

12. How do you know when your body needs rest or food? What signs do you notice?

13. Why is it important to take care of your body? How do you do that?

14. What are some activities that make you feel strong and healthy?

15. Ask your parents these same questions.

Chapter 7: By the Bend in the River

They spent all morning down by the river, fishing, swimming, exploring, and talking about all kinds of things.

Grandpa said that the pools that swirled in the river looked just the way he imagined the chakras.

Ethan and Lukas wanted to learn everything there was to know about fishing from grandpa, while Hudson was happiest just splashing around in puddles, looking for crabs and weird creatures, and building tiny huts and forts out of sticks and pebbles. Hudson loved getting his hands and feet full of mud and grass.

Grandpa showed them how to put a worm onto a fishing hook and how to tie the hook to the fishing line. Lukas wasn't very good at casting his fishing line yet, but in the end, he was the only one who caught a fish, and a big one too.

At first, he wanted to take it home for dinner, but grandpa said it was better if they put it back in the river because they had plenty of fish at home already. Lukas agreed with a sigh, though he wasn't happy, and they set the fish free.

"Bye, little silverfish," said Hudson. "Kolakesh says he hopes the hook didn't hurt you."

Ethan and Lukas smiled at their little brother.

"You say the strangest things, Hudson!" said Ethan, "It's one of the many reasons why I love you."

Grandpa was wading in the shallow river, trying to free a line that had gotten snagged. He was standing on a large rock that was slightly underwater. Suddenly his foot slipped because the rock was very smooth and slippery, and he went back-first into the water with a yell and a loud splash!

The boys looked up, startled, and ran to the spot where their grandpa had fallen into the river.

All three boys were strong swimmers and very comfortable in the water. Their parents had gotten them swimming lessons each year since they were babies. The brothers knew how to swim fast, how to swim underwater, how to hold their breath, and how to find their way back to the surface if they dived deep.

They were about to dive in after their grandfather, but after a moment, they saw his head come up out of the water. He was quite a distance from where he had fallen in. They watched him slowly swim back to shore as they ran over to help him.

Water streamed down his grey beard and coat. His hat was forever lost down the river, and he was completely soaked!

"Boys," he sputtered as he slowly climbed back onto the shore and sat on the grass to catch his breath, "I need a little help. I hit my feet against that rock as I fell in. Find me a good thick stick I can use for support. There are several fallen branches around us that will make good walking sticks."

Lukas quickly got up to find the best sticks he could for grandpa while Hudson and Ethan collected their fishing gear, packing it back up and getting ready to go back home. They were a little worried because they'd never seen their grandpa fall or have an accident. The sudden way he had fallen into the water had shaken them up.

Lukas ran back with two sturdy branches grandpa could use as walking sticks for support.

"We were so worried about you, grandpa!" mumbled little Hudson as he hugged him tightly around the neck, his lower lip quivering with emotion.

"I'm ok Hudsy," whispered grandpa. I was lucky, there is an undercurrent in the river that you can't see on the surface. When I fell in it swept me farther downstream. Luckily, it wasn't very strong and I know how to swim."

"We were about to jump in after you, grandpa," said Lukas.

"I'm glad you didn't. That undercurrent could have been dangerous. It's always best to get to know the water first before jumping in - especially if you aren't familiar with it. You need to know how deep it is and where the depth changes, if there is an undercurrent, and what kinds of sea creatures live in it. This knowledge will help keep you safe and ensure you have a good time in the water if you decide to go in.

Ethan helped his grandpa stand up while Lukas passed him a branch. Grandpa took two steps and stopped, he closed his eyes and inhaled deeply.

"Kids," he began, "I'm afraid I won't be able to walk back home. It seems I've hit my feet so hard on the rocks that I can't put my weight onto them, even with the help of the walking sticks."

Grandpa Otto sat down quietly, thinking. There was no way to call for help because in the forest there was no telephone signal, and even if there was, his mobile phone was wet as it had also fallen into the river. He tried several times to start it up but it wouldn't. This was a good lesson about keeping your electronics safely stored and far away from water.

"Ethan, you'll have to go back home and take everyone with you. Tell grandma or Aunt Yvette to bring the truck," Grandpa groaned slightly, gently rubbing his foot and ankle.

"Do you boys remember the dirt road we passed on the way to the river? asked grandpa.

"Yes," they all nodded.

"Go back to the dirt road and head home in the same direction we came. You boys will find your way back to the house without me, don't worry. Just follow the river until the bend, you'll see the dirt road and path from there. Make sure to stick together and go straight home."

Grandpa really struggled with this decision; he didn't feel comfortable letting the kids go back alone, but he also didn't want Ethan walking home by himself while their brothers waited with him. The kids had been to the river with him a few times before, so he felt confident that they would find their way. He knew that in the future, they would have to find some good back-up plans for unexpected events such as this.

Root Chakra Discussion Questions

1. Have you ever become lost? Were you scared?

2. How could you get help if you are lost? What would you do?

3. Do you know your address and your parents' phone numbers by heart?
   Can you recite this information out loud now?

4. Imagine that someone younger than you feels afraid – how can you help
   them handle that emotion? What would you say to them?

5. What do your parents do when you are afraid of something? Do they give
   you a hug, read your favourite bedtime story, or do something else?
   What do you wish they would do or say?

6. How do you feel when you're in a new place you aren't familiar with?
   Do you have a special item or something familiar that helps you feel more
   comfortable?

7. Can you describe a time when you were really brave?
   What helped you be brave in that situation?

8. When a fish gets caught, it flaps around wildly, trying to get away and back
   into the water. The fish doesn't feel safe, and its instincts kick in, trying to
   save its life. That is a Root Chakra response. Do you think fish have feelings?

9. Ask your parents these same questions.

It was settled. The three boys and Kolakesh had to walk back home without grandpa. Ethan was the oldest, so he was in charge. He was fairly certain he remembered the way.

They walked back along the river until they found where it curved. All four of them looked back to where their grandpa was sitting on the grass. Grandpa smiled and waved to them. They waved back, then turned left and walked on, leaving their grandpa alone. Ethan, Lukas, Hudson, and Kolakesh all felt really badly leaving him behind. Neither of them liked this and wished they could have found another way to bring him along. They loved their grandpa, felt worried about him, and anxious to get him help as soon as possible.

Soon they saw the dirt road grandpa had mentioned. It was the path that would lead them through the woods. It was late afternoon and the sun was low in the sky. The shadows were growing deeper, and everything looked different from the way it had earlier in the day. It all seemed creepy and unfamiliar now. What if they got lost in the woods?

"Come on, we have to move," said Ethan. "I think it's less than an hour from here. Do you need to rest, Hudson?"

"No, I'm good," he replied happily. "Kolakesh looks a bit tired, though, and he says we should take another path."

"There isn't another path." Said Ethan. "Besides, grandpa said we were to take this one."

So the boys continued bravely on into the darkening forest. It was overgrown and smelled of moss and trees and mushrooms and rotting wood. Even the chirping of the birds sounded eerie.

The path became narrow and winding so the boys began to walk one behind the other.

Suddenly, Hudson shouted: "Stop! Kolakesh says there's danger!"

"What kind of danger?" asked Lukas with wide eyes. "Is it a wildcat?"

"No – I don't know," replied Hudson, "but Kolakesh speaks to the trees and birds, and they're warning him about something on the path in front of us."

Carefully the boys crept forward, and as they got around the next bend in the path – they heard it.

A sharp rattling sound.

"What's that?" Screeched Lukas in a strained whisper.

Suddenly, the sound of twigs breaking and leaves shifting around on the ground hit their ears, as if the weight of something was crushing them.

Ethan took a deep breath and put his hand up to stop everyone from moving forward.

The sun was getting even lower in the sky and the forest became darker. Only here and there could you see the remaining sunlight shining through to the forest floor.

"Let's stay still while we look around," he said as calmly as he could.

Lukas opened his mouth to say something but no sound came out because that was the precise moment when he saw it.

"What is it, Lukas?!" asked Ethan, noticing his brother's strange expression.

Lukas simply pointed.

There was a great, big rattlesnake curled up in a patch of sunlight looking directly at the three brothers with its tongue out, hissing slightly. The rattlesnake was blocking the path and there was no way around it because the path was narrow with steep rocks on both sides. The snake had its head raised, continued to hiss, and began to rattle its tail. The boys froze on the spot, feeling very nervous.

"What should we do?" Lukas asked in a small, scared voice. "I think we should run…." He was standing behind Ethan, holding tightly onto his brother's sleeve.

Chapter 9: Facing Your Fears

"Let's all back away slowly," said Ethan. He was surprised at how calm his voice sounded. Hudson and Lukas were terrified. They were ready to run all the way back down to the river to grandpa, but Ethan held them back.

To be honest, Ethan was afraid too. The only other time he had seen a rattlesnake this close was in a reptile park – and that one was behind glass. There was no way they could turn back now – grandpa needed help, and it was getting late.

"We have to be brave," Ethan said, "Just like we've been practising. Remember, as grandpa said, the snake doesn't really want to harm us – it's scared too. Still, the snake can be dangerous, so we have to be careful not to frighten it even more, or get into its way. I'm going to try to talk to it and ask it to move. Let's all back up even further just to be safe."

The three brave boys (and the wise Kolakesh) faced their fears together. They stood at a safe distance from the snake, and then Ethan spoke as calmly as he could.

"Hello, Mr. Snake. Or – um – Mrs. Snake. My name's Ethan, and these are my brothers, Lukas and Hudson. The invisible guy over there is Kolakesh. We're sorry to have disturbed you..."

The snake looked at them and rattled, continuing to stick out its tongue and hiss at the boys.

"We don't want to hurt you or bother you – but – "Ethan looked around at the thick forest and impossible rocks on all sides – "We really need to use this pathway. Otherwise, we might get lost, and our grandpa needs help."

The rattlesnake moved its head this way and that way, tasting the air with its flickering tongue. Ethan knelt down so he wouldn't look so tall and scary to a snake.

"Let's throw a stick at it," whispered Lukas.

"No, wait. Give it a moment," whispered Ethan. "If we scare it even more, it may think we are trying to hurt it. Remember what grandpa said about scared animals - they may attack humans. Let's be safe and keep our distance while sending soothing thoughts to it."

Ethan kept talking to the snake gently, with as much courage and friendliness as he could muster. His palms were sweaty, and his nerves were just about to give out.

But he kept talking softly and gently.

Lukas tried too. "Please don't bite us, Mr. Snake. We respect you…"
Hudson added: "I like snakes… and you are a very beautiful snake.
Kolakesh likes you too."

They talked and talked for a long time – saying all kinds of silly things in the
end – until finally – the rattlesnake stopped hissing and slithered away.

Without so much as a backward glance, it slid into the bushes and
dispeared. For a long time, the boys waited there, just to make sure it was
really gone. They were all still a bit shaken – but now the feeling
was different.

Ethan thought to himself: "So this is what it feels like to face your fears…"

"Kolakesh says it's safe." Said Hudson, although he didn't sound very
convinced.

At last, the boys got the courage to run past the spot where the snake had
been curled up, and they kept running most of the way back as fast as
Hudson's shorter legs could go.

"Look, there's the house!" Ethan pointed triumphantly to grandma and
grandpa's farmhouse. Without thinking too much about the path back after
they passed the rattlesnake, their muscle memory had gotten them safely
home without fully realizing how they had gotten there.

Aunt Yvette was outside her yurt planting some mint as they ran up to her,
out of breath, and trying to talk at the same time.

"Whoa, slow down everybody," she said as she patiently waited for them to calm down and catch their breath.

"Grandpa had an accident! He fell into the river and hurt himself. He can't walk and needs us to bring him back in the truck! We need to go right away, Aunt Yvette, let's go!" Ethan was grabbing her hand and hurriedly leading her to the truck when she stopped him.

"Ethan, before we go, tell me all the details so I know what we need to bring with us besides blankets and homeopathic remedies," she said, then hugged him, Lukas, and Hudson.

Suddenly, each one took long deep breaths and had some tears flow out of their eyes. The boys hadn't realized just how shaken up they were, and only now that they had reached the first goal of getting back home alone, were they able to relax a little. Their body showed the release of that tension with little shakes and tears - a completely normal response.

Aunt Yvette hugged them tightly and told them not to worry; if grandpa sent them home alone he knew they would make it and that he would be ok until help arrived.

"Lukas and Hudson, go into the house and tell grandma what happened. She will know what to do next. You can help her."

"Ethan, I will get some supplies then you and I will go get grandpa. I think I know which part of the river he is at."

"Boys," Aunt Yvette stepped closer to look at each one of her nephews, "I'm proud of you for making it back on your own. I know it was hard for you to leave grandpa and also to go through the forest by yourselves." You did everything right, exactly as grandpa told you to."

The boys nodded, relaxing a little. Lukas and Hudson ran to the house to find Grandma Suzan. Aunt Yvette and Ethan quickly packed some supplies, got into the truck, and headed back into the forest to find Grandpa.

Grandma Suzan began preparing a healing poultice made from herbs that are good for sprains. It included comfrey, arnica, turmeric, and willow bark. She gathered all the herbs in a mortar and pestle and began to mash them together. She then added a little water and mixed it all together into a thick, medicinal paste.

Once the poultice was ready, Grandma Suzan went back to her garden to collect more herbs to make grandpa a soothing tea that included more comfrey and arnica, as well as chamomile, valerian, and ashwagandha.

Lukas, Hudson, and Kolakesh were silently watching her every move, taking it all in. They wanted to help, too, so Grandma Suzan had them take turns mashing the herbs together with the mortar and pestle. She began humming a happy tune under her breath when Lukas suddenly asked how she could be happy when grandpa was injured and not home yet.

Wasn't she worried about him?

"Yes, of course, sweetheart; I felt very worried when you first told me what happened, Lukas. In fact, I am still a little worried, but I won't let that get me down in the dumps because that won't help grandpa or us," she explained with a smile.

"I reflected on the fact that you boys did everything right, and you made it home exactly as grandpa told you to. I know your aunt and brother will bring him home very soon. In the meantime, do you think it will help if we become fearful and put fearful energy into this healing medicine we are making for grandpa?"

"I know we are supposed to put happy, loving energy into the things we make for people," began Lukas, "but how can I do that when he is out there alone in the woods, and it's getting dark? Anything can happen! What if snakes find him, or if he gets too cold, or, or…" began Lukas with a sob.

"You are right about all those things, Lukas; however, that is our imagination getting the better of us. We can't allow that to happen. While it's good to think about the many things that can happen so we can prepare for them in the future, you can't allow that kind of thinking to overwhelm you, making you feel so anxious that you freeze up or drive your energy down. Whenever you find yourself in a difficult or worrisome situation, try to keep your energies up while preparing to improve the situation in ways that you can control. If you can't change the situation right away, do your best to make your peace with it while you figure out a way to change it."

"The best thing for all of us to do is to prepare this medicine with as much love as possible, so these healing poultices, teas, and meals for grandpa will help him recover his strength and ground his body and mind more quickly."

"If the injury is more serious, we will get help at the hospital, then help him recover at home," grandma added while preparing a strong medicinal tea for grandpa.

"Doesn't it feel good when your mom or dad kisses a part of your body you've hurt?" asked Grandma Suzan.

"Yes. It really does feel better," responded Lukas, thinking about the other day when he fell off his bike and landed on his arm. After his mom kissed it, his arm really did start to feel better. It was like magic.

"It's the same for everyone," explained Grandma Suzan. "When someone does something kind, to help you feel better, that kindness, that loving energy is the "secret ingredient" that combines with whatever you did to make it even more powerful."

"You know, when a person has a shock, such as unexpectedly falling into ice-cold water or hurting themselves, their entire Self - their mind, body, and energy bodies - all feel tight, contracted, and uprooted. That person can fall out of alignment. While that is a normal response meant to help keep you alive until you reach safety because it sharpens your senses in a way that allows you to focus on what you need to be safe, it's also good to do things that help to soothe and relax both your body and mind afterward. That way, the negative memories of that shock don't stay in your energy field. Even if it's a memory later on, you won't feel bad when you occasionally remember what happened."

"That's called working through your feelings and releasing them. People store memories and feelings in their bodies - both the physical and energetic bodies - and when those feelings don't feel good, they can cause imbalance and sickness in the mind or body."

"That's why it's important to work through strong feelings and not get caught up in them in an endless spiral."

Lukas and Hudson nodded. Even Kolakesh nodded, but only Hudson saw him do it.

"OK, boys, tell me about the most fun things you've done this summer." Quizzed Grandma Suzan.

She knew that if she got them talking about happy things, they would be able to change their feelings and energy. Once they were smiling and happily chatting, she gave them the mortar and pestle again and told them to put as much happy energy into the mixture as they could by focusing their love and joy into what they were doing, knowing that it would help grandpa feel better.

"Now boys, we are not pretending that nothing happened. Hiding from the truth is not the way to handle strong emotions, but you need to know how not to get sucked into a negative spiral of despair or fear."

"We understand, grandma," chimed in Hudson. Lukas smiled and nodded too, as he mashed more herbs together in the mortar and pestle.

They intuitively felt that what their grandmother told them was true. Being sad when someone is sad or angry doesn't help them feel better. Glowing with light and sometimes even cracking some ridiculous jokes often helps people feel much better.

"Did you boys know that your Aunt Yvette broke her knee when she was younger?"

"Really?" Lukas and Hudson asked in unison with surprise in their eyes.

"Really," explained grandma. "She fell and broke her kneecap into hundreds of tiny pieces. To make it worse, this was right before she was scheduled to fly to China to visit a sacred mountain range called Wudang and train at the famous Shaolin temple."

"Woooowwww," whispered the boys in unison. They had no idea their aunt had broken a bone, or gone to China.

"Before she went in for surgery, your grandpa went in to talk with her. I don't know what he said, but before long, I could hear them howling with laughter! They laughed so hard they both had tears coming out of their eyes - at least that's what your aunt told me later. Pretty soon, even the nurses and doctors were laughing too. They said that no one ever laughs before surgery. People are so serious and sad or upset, but not your aunt and grandpa. They had the entire room laughing right along with them. Everyone was in good spirits even though they had a serious surgery ahead of them. Laughing also enabled your aunt to create happy, healing chemicals in her body that helped her heal faster. Did you know that the most powerful pharmacy in the world is your mind? That's right. We have the ability to create potent chemicals in our bodies that relieve pain, make us feel good, and much more - all by creating certain emotions. You can create specific emotions by choosing to think certain thoughts that trigger those feelings."

"So you see, keeping a light and cheerful disposition has many positives, plus, it's a nice way to encourage the people around you to feel uplifted too."

"Grandma," began Lukas, "did Aunt Yvette make it to that mountain range in China?"

"Yes, she did, sweetheart, and many others after. Maybe one day she'll tell you about it," replied Grandma Suzan mysteriously with a smile.

Ethan and Aunt Yvette reached grandpa just as the last rays of sun were beginning to fade.

"We made it grandpa! We found you!" Exclaimed Ethan proudly as he ran to his grandfather and gave him a big hug. Grandpa Otto wrapped his arms around Ethan and hugged him back.

"I knew you would Ethan. Thank you", he whispered with genuine gratitude as he closed his eyes and held his grandson even closer.

"You and your brothers did great, as I knew you would," he whispered in Ethan's ear, proud of his grandsons.

Aunt Yvette and Ethan helped grandpa into the truck after wrapping warm blankets around him and giving him some water with electrolytes and homeopathic drops to help his body relax and overcome the shock from the accident.

Pretty soon, they were home and the whole family came out to help him get into the house.

After a good look, it seemed his ankles were sprained but nothing looked broken. Everyone was happy to be safe and back together again.

Root Chakra Discussion Questions

1. Is there something that you were once afraid of that doesn't bother you anymore? How did you get over that fear?

2. Have you faced any of your fears? What did you do?

3. Have you seen someone else face their fears? How did they do it?

4. Have you noticed that your feelings and thoughts are connected? Thoughts have vibrations and can uplift you and make you feel good or bad. Wouldn't you rather choose thoughts that feel good?

5. Do you ever talk to yourself in your head or out loud? Do you speak with yourself lovingly and kindly, or do you choose thoughts and words that don't feel good? Say out loud what you usually think to yourself in your head. How does it sound and feel to you? Do you want to change your thoughts? If so, what do you prefer?

6. Do you enjoy being alone every now and then? What is the best thing about it?

7. Have you ever met a snake? What do you think you should do if you see one in the woods?

8. Ask your parents these same questions.

Chapter 10: Home Base

It was late afternoon the next day. Grandpa had slept 12 hours! His body needed extra time to rest and heal. He woke up late, had a light lunch, then lay down again for another rest.

The sun was gracefully setting over the mountains and the forest. All was well, and there was peace.

Long, lazy sunbeams turned the clouds red, meaning that it would be windy the next day. It was a good day for the Root Chakra and the chakra of the brave. At least, that's what Kolakesh said as he played a tune on his snout as if it were a flute.

Ethan's mom and dad had driven over to the farm early in the morning to visit for the weekend and see how grandpa was doing. The whole family gathered around the dinner table as Grandma Suzan finished making a fresh batch of their favorite family treat - palachinta.

Grandpa was awake again and slowly made his way over to the table with the help of Ethan's dad, Tom.

Everyone was talking about how the boys had faced their greatest fears and what they had learned about themselves in the process.

Grandpa sat at the head of the table with his leg propped up on a pillow. He was smiling. His ankles had a long white cloth wrapped around them. It smelled like one of Grandma Suzan's herbal ointments - and it was. Inside the white cloth was the herbal poultice the boys helped her make for him. It helped bring down the swelling while reducing the pain. Grandpa was also sipping a fresh cup of herbal tea, and feeling pretty good, even though his ankles hurt a little.

Grandpa was relaxed and feeling grateful for all the good in his life, like his family. He helped himself speed up the healing process by imagining himself perfect, his ankle completely healed, and running through the fields barefoot with his grandkids, laughing. He briefly closed his eyes as he imagined how good it felt to run through the fields like that, feeling strong, healthy, and absolutely fantastic. He could practically feel his ankle smiling with happy knowing and anticipation at that memory.

Hudson suddenly burst out, "Kolakesh says that memories can happen in the past or the future, is that true?" he asked.

Grandpa smiled at Hudson and nodded. "That's right. In fact, I am enjoying a future memory right now. I imagine it into the present moment, bringing that experience closer to me by visualising how it feels when it happens. I pretend it has already happened and let myself enjoy the feelings of it already happening. It's one of the great secrets to creating whatever you want in life. If you want something, you must imagine how good it feels right now as if you already have it or are it. You need to fully imagine yourself enjoying it, feeling it, and living it as if it is happening now."

With a mischievous grin, Grandma Suzan pretended to be angry with grandpa for letting the boys walk home alone. That didn't stop her from fussing over him with great care.

Ethan turned to his family with a big, contented smile, and said, "You know, so much of what happened these past few days reminds me of the lessons of the first chakra."

"You are right, Ethan," smiled Aunt Yvette.

Grandpa then added with a thoughtful nod of his head, "The roots of family connect us and keep us safe during life's storms. As do the thoughts we choose to think and the feelings we create within ourselves. It's up to us to decide how we handle unexpected situations and the thoughts and feelings that pop up with them."

The blue Wellington boots now stand on the porch because Lukas, Hudson, Kolakesh, and Ethan are all running barefoot on the farm these days. They enjoy grounding themselves whenever they can by getting as close to Mother Earth as possible, swimming in the lake, walking through the grass without shoes, spending time with their favourite trees - telling them their stories, thoughts, and feelings, and helping grandma care for the plants in her garden.

They also learned how to help Aunt Yvette in the bee yard. In the evenings, when they were all in her yurt looking up at the stars and night sky through the hole in the top, she told them many stories about her travels, the secrets of Wudang and the Shaolin temple, and began teaching them internal and external martial arts, breathing and meditation techniques, and yoga asanas. She always had dozens of questions for them about all kinds of fascinating topics. Usually, they were about things they had never thought about until she asked them. They loved those evening talks!

In the afternoons, they went with grandpa into the forest, where they learned about the many animals in the area. They began to understand the secret language of the animals based on how they acted. They could then decipher the secret codes that told everyone around them that there was danger up ahead or food nearby. It was truly amazing to see how incredibly wise and knowing mother nature and all her children are. It was the humans who needed to relearn, to remember how to understand their natural world again.

It was the summer of learning, and they loved every moment of it! The memories of those days went deep into their spirits, grounding them, becoming happy memories they would enjoy for the rest of their lives - and perhaps, many other lifetimes, too.

The End

What Do You Think About The Second Book?

Friends, we have come to the end of book 2.
How did you like it? What did you most enjoy about the story?

I'd love to hear about your favourite parts and welcome you to
share them with me via email at: feedback@singingsoulbooks.com

As a gift to you, dear reader, here is a sneak peak of the first two chapters
of book 3. Enjoy!

Loving appreciation to all that you are and bring to the world.
Keep shining your light!

Warmly,

Yvette

Book Three:
Finding Your Place in the Team
Exploring the Sacral Chakra

Chapter One: What's it Like to be a Bee?

The first thing Ethan remembered about his dream was the loud buzzing. The droning noise filled his head and made him feel quite odd. His entire body reverberated with the sound. Everything he looked at seemed a lot bigger than it should have been. Floating in the air, all around Ethan, were hundreds of them.

So many bees! They were all buzzing around, going this way and that. Each bee was doing its own thing, and yet somehow, all of them knew exactly what to do and where to go. Not one bee bumped into another, even though they seemed to be flying in dozens of directions at once. It was quite dizzying to watch.

They had large dark eyes and hairy bodies with black and yellow stripes. It looked like they were wearing fuzzy flying pajamas covered in gold dust.

The strangest thing of all was that 10-year-old Ethan knew he was a bee too. Somehow, that made him very happy, and he smiled to himself.

"I must be dreaming," he thought, and then, just as he realized that it was a dream – lickety-split – he completely forgot again.

The bees were leaving the hive and heading towards a big open patch of sun nearby.

Bee-Ethan sniffed the air.

There was an enchanting smell… sniff…sniff…

It was coming from where the warm, golden streaks of sunlight hit the patch of green just in front of a thick forest of trees. Everyone was heading that way. So, without even having to think about how or where to fly, Ethan flapped his bee wings like mad, and away he zoomed, following his nose, along with all the other bees, heading straight toward that delicious smell.

The trees looked enormous – like giant skyscrapers. They made his head spin when he looked up.

Far down below, a mile away, it seemed, there was a big, perfectly round, white and black object. It looked to be about the size of a big house. Ethan couldn't make out what it was, so he just followed the other bees. It was enormous fun, zigging and zagging all over the garden.

The flowers were as big as swimming pools. Something inside Bee-Ethan really wanted to go explore those flowers.

He saw a big, blue flower nearby. It had the most mesmerizing yellow spots on its petals. It looked like the other bees were having a party there. To his surprise, as soon as Bee-Ethan tried to join them, he found that he couldn't get there. He flapped and flapped – but it was no use. He was stuck. He just couldn't fly any closer.

Try as he might, he couldn't get to that tempting blue flower and the golden pollen party. The scene began to fade away. Something was calling to him. It sounded far away at first, then more insistent.

"Ethan!", came a loud call from downstairs, "you're going to be late for school. Get yourself down here!"

Ethan had overslept that morning.

He felt a little frustrated and disappointed when he woke up. He really wanted to join in the pollen party with the other bees.

Chapter Two: Stuck on the Bench

Ethan and his younger brother, Lukas, had soccer practice after school. Lukas, who played on the junior team, ran faster than others his age and loved showing off his skills with the ball. The coach selected him as the striker because nine times out of ten, Lukas could kick the ball straight into the back of the net.

The only thing the coach complained about was that Lukas didn't like to pass the ball to anyone else on the team. He was a soccer ball hog.

"You can't win the match on your own, Lukas," said the coach. "Soccer is a team sport. Pass the ball!"

Ethan, who was on the senior team, wasn't quite as sporty as his younger brother. He wasn't the fastest runner, and he had the habit of being too cautious. Ethan didn't like to take risks. He preferred reading books and drawing to playing sports. This year was the first time he had tried out for any kind of team, persuaded by his mom, who thought he should try something different and outside his comfort zone.

So far, things were not going his way. 'Different' was no fun. There was a match coming up, and more than likely, Ethan would spend a lot of time on the bench again. The coach said he could try again in a couple of weeks and that he just needed more practice.

He tried very, very hard to fit in with the team. He always tried to be the kind of person he thought they would like, but still, he felt like an outsider. The other boys thought he was just weird, shy, and goofy. They actually believed that Ethan liked sitting on the bench. It was all a big joke to them.

Practice that afternoon was no different for poor Ethan. He was the last one over the finish line during the warm-up. He missed completely when it was his turn to kick a goal into the net. He couldn't stop the ball dead when someone passed to him, and it seemed like the coach was giving him a hard time.

The other boys on the team called him "Wumzie" (short for "Clumsy-Wumsy") because of the way he fumbled the soccer ball.

By the time the two boys got home, Ethan was in a foul mood.

To be continued...

Root Chakra Song for Children

Down at the base of my spine,
A glowing light that's red and fine,
It's my root, my grounding place,
It keeps me steady, and sets my pace.

Muladhara, I feel strong,
Rooted deep, where I belong,
With the Earth, I feel secure,
In my heart, I know for sure.

Trust and courage, they are mine,
Safe and sound, I feel just fine,
I have enough, I am complete,
With my root, I am strong on my feet.

Muladhara, I feel strong,
Rooted deep, where I belong,
With the Earth, I feel secure,
In my heart, I know for sure.

LAM, I chant, it brings me peace,
Grounding me, my fears release,
I am cherished, I am whole,
My happy root chakra, makes me bold.

Muladhara, I feel strong,
Rooted deep, where I belong,
With the Earth, I feel secure,
In my heart, I know for sure.

I am safe, I am sound,
With my root, I'm always found,
Loved and whole, perfect and neat,
With my root, I am complete.

Muladhara, I feel strong,
Rooted deep, where I belong,
With the Earth, I feel secure,
In my heart, I know for sure.

Yvette Farkas

Yvette is the creator of Singing Soul Books and a magical story enchantress. She can often be found wandering the deepest sanctuaries of forests and mountains and enjoying the "thundering loud" quiet of sacred spaces both outside and within.

She enjoys sharing her love of the unusual and mystical such as bullwhip cracking, foraging for herbs while the dew is still fresh, harnessing the power of natural energies, telling captivating stories in her yurt, and sharing wisdom gleaned from 30+ years of training in the martial and healing arts.

Yvette is an explorer of consciousness, a writer, gardener, photographer, traveller, and a budding beekeeper. She is a child of the Universe, leaving seeds of joy and the sweet aroma of empowered belief in the people she meets while learning and growing.

Yvette is also a health-based, heart-centered coach and mentor, and a practitioner of ancient healing practices taking people back to their health and their hearts. She uses the power of stories to share love and wisdom and reveal the inherent interconnectedness of all things, inspiring and empowering others toward their highest potential. Her work is meant to shed light on that which people rarely see, to uplift their Spirits, forge deep heartfelt connections, and inspire their hearts.

You can reach Yvette here:

www.singingsoulbooks.com, www.yvettefarkas.com and www.bioresonancescans.com
LinkedIn: https://www.linkedin.com/in/yvettefarkas

Jana Rothwell

Jana is the illustrator of Singing Soul Books. She finds passion in using her endless imagination to teach and create art that captivates people of all ages. She strives to empower others to grow, to learn to love themselves unconditionally, to speak their truth and to follow their dreams. She enjoys exploring the beauty in nature and feels most at home near and in the water. Jana encompasses all the character-istics of a typical Pisces: she is creative, gentle, sensitive, kind, compassionate, intuitive, and wise. Infinite amounts of light and love radiate from her. She connects deeply with children and animals because of their innocence and pure hearts.

She has the unique ability of seeing the best and the potential in everyone she meets. As a strong believer in the vastness and power of the Universe, Jana embraces the idea that we are all connected. She is a free spirit, continually learning and growing, always ready to share her creative ideas and stories, and never afraid to laugh at her own silliness.

You can reach Jana here:

janarothwelldesigns.com
Email: info@janarothwell.com
Instagram: @janalee_111 and @marigold_creative_art

Wayne Bloemhof

Wayne is a piece of the infinite creative wonder that just is. He claims nothing special as his own, always amazed at the words that come out of his fingertips as he types. Where do they come from? We can only speculate.

He lives in a place called Knysna, which is a little piece of heaven. He feeds the Turacos and white-eyes, sharing his apples, oranges and bananas with the forest creatures.

He often just walks down to the river, for no reason in particular, and leads a quiet life of wonder. He writes, ghostwrites and creates to help
people put words to the stories in their hearts.

You can reach Wayne here:
www.waynebloemhof.wordpress.com
Email: waynebloemhof@gmail.com

Resources

Glossary for the second book:

Spiritual, metaphysical, and unusual terms and their meanings from the second book in the "Ethan and the Seven Chakras" book series.

1. **Alternate Nostril Breathing:** A breathing exercise that involves alternating the breathing between the left and right nostrils to balance the brain and improve mental clarity.
2. **Asana:** A term used to describe the practice of yoga postures. Asanas also mean "a pose you can comfortably hold for a long time."
3. **Awakening:** Process of becoming aware of spiritual and metaphysical concepts and the potential within oneself.
4. **Cabin Fever:** A feeling of restlessness, irritability, or boredom that occurs when a person is stuck indoors for an extended period.
5. **Chakras:** Energy centres in the body, corresponding to different physical, emotional, and spiritual aspects of a person's being. There are seven main chakras in a line along a person's spine: the root chakra, sacral chakra, solar plexus chakra, heart chakra, throat chakra, third eye chakra, and crown chakra.
6. **Consciousness:** The state of being aware of one's surroundings, thoughts, and feelings. It involves actively recognising and comprehending the state of existence.
7. **Divine Spirit:** A spiritual concept that refers to the inner essence of a person that is pure, perfect, and divine.
8. **Emotions:** Complex psychological states that involve a mix of chemicals and hormones the brain makes to create physiological stimuli. Emotions are fundamental to the human experience, influencing thoughts, behaviours, and overall well-being.
9. **Energy:** The force that sustains and animates all living things and is believed to exist in different forms and frequencies.

10. **Essence:** The fundamental nature or intrinsic quality of something.

11. **Hanuman:** A Hindu deity considered a symbol of strength, devotion, and loyalty.

12. **Innate Wisdom:** The intuitive and natural understanding a person has about themselves and the world around them.

13. **Intuition:** The ability to know or understand something without needing conscious reasoning or proof. An impression or insight gained by this faculty.

14. **Introspection:** The examination of one's thoughts and feelings.

15. **Meditation:** A practice or mental exercise in which an individual focuses on a particular object, thought, or activity to achieve a mentally clear and emotionally calm state and become aware of one's thoughts and feelings.

16. **Metaphysical:** Refers to concepts or ideas beyond the physical world or empirical reality.

17. **Mindful Eating:** A practice of paying attention to the present moment while eating, chewing food well, enjoying the flavours in each bite, and appreciating the blessings of life.

18. **Mindfulness**: A state of active, open attention to the present moment without judgment or distraction.

19. **Pineal Gland:** A small endocrine gland in the brain that produces and regulates hormones, including melatonin, associated with spiritual and mystical experiences.

20. **Salivary Glands:** Three kinds of glands in different areas of the mouth that squirt saliva when needed.

21. **Seeds of Knowledge:** When nurtured, small pieces of information or insight can grow and expand into more profound understanding.

22. **Self-love:** Honouring one's needs. Showing oneself compassion and appreciation, setting boundaries and being able to say "no" or "yes."

23. **Zen Moment:** A state of mind in which a person becomes fully absorbed in the present moment, letting go of past and future concerns and achieving a sense of inner peace and clarity.

Palachinta Recipe (spelled "palacsinta" in Hungarian)

Curious to taste the delicious dessert that Grandma Suzan made Ethan and the kids in the story? Here it is! Make these special Hungarian crepes yourself and share them with your loved ones.

These pancakes are large in diameter and very thin, unlike their North American cousins which are smaller in diameter yet thick.

The thin size of Hungarian crepes enables you to spread jam, cottage cheese, chocolate, nuts, or other foods on the crepe, and then roll it up for eating. You can also pour maple syrup, freshly made chocolate sauce, or other treats onto the rolled-up crepes.

Equipment:

- Mixing bowls
- Measuring cups
- Whisk
- Non-stick frying pan
- Spatula
- Fork
- Ladle
- Plates

Ingredients:

Batter
- 2 whole eggs
- 1 1/4 cups all-purpose flour
- 1 1/4 cups almond, oat, or other milk
- 2/3 cup sparkling water
- 1 pinch salt
- 1 teaspoon sugar
- Oil/fat for frying

Cottage cheese filling:
- 1 egg yolk
- 2/3 cup dry cottage cheese or ricotta
- 1/2 lemon zest
- 1 teaspoon vanilla extract
- 1 tablespoon sugar
- Mix, spread on crepe, roll up, and eat.

Walnut filling:
- Ground walnuts
- Sugar
- 2:1 ratio of walnuts to sugar (some people prefer a 1:1 ratio, adjust to your preference)

Instructions:

- Mix all ingredients except the
  sparkling water. Ensure there
  are no lumps in the batter.

- When smooth, add the
  sparkling water and mix.

- The consistency should be
  similar to that of a yogurt drink.
  Not too runny yet not thick.

- Set a frying pan over medium heat.
  Add a few drops of oil. Once hot, fill the
  ladle with batter and pour it evenly onto the
  frying pan.

- Tilt the pan in all directions so the batter coats the surface of the pan
  completely. If you have holes in the palachinta, fill them with a little batter.

- Fry the underside of the palachinta until it is a light golden brown colour.
  Use a spatula to loosen it from the frying pan and check the underside to
  be sure it is a golden colour.

- Flip the pancake and fry the other side as well. When done, slide the crepe
  onto a plate and prepare the pan for the next ladle of batter.

- Stir the mixture each time before pouring it into the pan.

- Repeat until you have used up all the batter.

- Spread each pancake with jam, walnut filling, or cottage cheese filling.
  Roll up and enjoy eating with friends and family.

The Mystic's Library of Excellence

The Mystic's Library of Excellence is a treasure trove (organized topic-wise) for those seeking to dive deeper into the ideas explored in the "Ethan and the Seven Chakras" books.

Topics include sacred geometry, remote viewing, near-death experiences, longevity practices, divine feminine and divine masculine concepts, championship mindsets, epigenetics, practical metaphysics, natural health practices, parthenogenesis, quantum physics, shamanism, energy medicine, ESP, and finance smarts.

For a detailed list with links, visit: www.singingsoulbooks.com

Each topic is a gateway to understanding the profound and the extraordinary. May your exploration be edifying and enriching.

Mind and Practical Metaphysics:

1. **Dr. Joe Dispenza**

   • **Books:** *Breaking the Habit of Being Yourself, Becoming Supernatural* (and other books)

   • Dispenza's work focuses on neuroscience, epigenetics, and quantum physics. His programs, books, and retreats guide people to elevate beyond their old patterns and create new ones toward a healthy, happy life.

2. **José Silva**

   • **Book:** *The Silva Method*

   • Silva's landmark work uses hypnosis and mental training to awaken the human mind's hidden potential beyond the traditional five senses.

3. **Florence Scovel Shinn**

   • **Books:** *The Game of Life and How to Play It, Your Word is Your Wand, The Secret Door to Success, The Power of the Spoken Word*

   • Emphasises the power of positive thought, affirmations, and spiritual principles for success and fulfilment.

4. **Esther and Jerry Hicks**

   • **Books:** *Ask and It Is Given: Learning to Manifest Your Desires, The Astonishing Power of Emotions: Let Your Feelings Be Your Guide* (and other books)

   • Explores the law of attraction and provides practical guidance on manifesting desires.

5. **Zinovia Dushkova**

   • **Book:** *The Secret Book of Dzyan: Unveiling the Truth About the Oldest Manuscript in the World, Revelations of the Sun, The Teachings of the Heart* (and other books)

   • Renowned author and philosopher, Zinovia Dushkova, Ph.D., was named one of the "100 Most Spiritually Influential Living People in 2020" by Watkins Mind Body Spirit magazine. She has written over 60 books, inspiring readers with her profound insights into love, compassion, and spiritual transformation.

6. **Neville Goddard**

   • **Books:** *The Power of Imagination*

   • Goddard's work delves into the transformative power of imagination and how it shapes our reality.

7. **Joseph Murphy**

   • **Books:** *The Power of Your Subconscious Mind*

   • Murphy explores how the subconscious mind influences behaviour and offers techniques to harness its power for personal success.

8. **Napoleon Hill**

   • **Books:** *The Law of Success in Sixteen Lessons, Think and Grow Rich* (and other books)

   • A classic in personal development, Hill's book outlines principles for achieving success and wealth through positive thinking and goal-setting.

9. **Dale Carnegie**

   • **Books:** *How to Win Friends and Influence People*

   • Carnegie provides timeless advice on effective communication, building relationships, and influencing others positively.

10. **David J. Schwartz**

   - **Books:** *The Magic of Thinking Big*

   - Schwartz encourages thinking beyond conventional limits to achieve personal and professional success.

11. **Maxwell Maltz**

   - **Books:** *Psycho-cybernetics*

   - Maltz explores the connection between self-image, success, and creativity.

12. **Claude M. Bristol**

   - **Books:** *The Magic of Believing*

   - Bristol explores the power of belief and how it can shape one's destiny.

13. **Peter B. Kyne**

   - **Books:** *The Go-Getter*

   - Kyne's book imparts valuable lessons on determination and achieving goals.

14. **RHJ**

   - **Books:** *It Works: The Little Red Book*

   - A concise guide to the power of positive thinking and manifestation.

15. **Russell H. Conwell**

   - **Books:** *Acres of Diamonds*

   - Conwell's book emphasises finding opportunities in one's own environment and recognizing the value of what is already at hand.

16. **James Allen**

   - **Books:** *As a Man Thinketh*

   - Allen's classic explores the impact of thoughts on character and circumstances, emphasising personal responsibility.

17. **Zig Ziglar**

   - **Books:** *See You At The Top*

   - Ziglar's teachings focus on motivation, goal-setting, and achieving success with a positive mindset.

18. **David Sereda**

  • **Private Membership Group:** *The Inner Circle*

  • David Sereda offers a community, products, and programs for those seeking personal and spiritual growth.

19. **Shahiroz Walji**

  • **Metaphysical Hub**

  • Shahiroz Walji's Metaphysical Hub provides resources and community for exploring metaphysical concepts.

20. **Proctor Gallagher Institute**

  • The Proctor Gallagher Institute focuses on personal development, prosperity, and transforming paradigms for success.

21. **Marisa Peer**

  • Marisa Peer is a renowned hypnotherapist and speaker, offering insights into transformation and mental well-being. Particularly known for her work in overcoming feelings of not being enough.

22. **Paul McKenna**

  • Paul McKenna provides resources for personal development and self-improvement through hypnosis and neuro-linguistic programming.

Consciousness, Quantum Physics, and Epigenetics:

1. **David R. Hawkins**

  • **Books:** *Map of Consciousness, Power Vs. Force* (and other books)

  • Hawkins explores the levels of human consciousness with a map to understand spiritual growth.

2. **Bruce H. Lipton, Ph.D.**

  • **Books:** *The Biology Of Belief, The Honeymoon Effect, Spontaneous Evolution*

  • Lipton's work bridges biology and spirituality, exploring how beliefs shape biology and influence health (epigenetics).

3. **Jacob Liberman**

  • **Books:** *Take Off Your Glasses and See: A Mind/Body Approach to Expanding Your Eyesight and Insight, Light: Medicine of the Future* (and other books)

  • Liberman combines a mind/body approach to vision, linking eyesight to broader insights and consciousness.

4. **Dr. Valerie V. Hunt**

  • **Books + DVDs:** *Infinite Mind: Science of the Human Vibrations of Consciousness, Uncork Your Consciousness* (and other books and DVDs)

  • Dr. Hunt delves into the science of human vibrations and their connection to consciousness.

5. **Dr. Konstantin Korotkov**

  • **Books:** T*he Energy of Consciousness, Light After Life: Experiments and Ideas on After-Death Changes of Kirlian Pictures* (and other books)

  • Korotkov explores the scientific aspects of human energy fields and their relationship to consciousness.

6. **Dr. Joe Dispenza**

  • **Books:** *Becoming Supernatural, Breaking the Habit of Being Yourself*

  (and other books)

  • Dr. Joe Dispenza's work (books, courses, retreats) explores epigenetics.

7. **Gary Zukav**

  • **Books:** *Dancing Wu Li Masters: An Overview of the New Physics, The Seat of the Soul* (and other books)

  • Zukav explores the new physics, bridging science and spirituality.

8. **Fritjof Capra**

  • **Books:** *The Tao of Physics, The Turning Point* (and other books)

  • Capra explores parallels between modern physics and Eastern mysticism, highlighting the interconnectedness of science and spirituality.

1. **Paul H. Smith**

- **Book:** *The Essential Guide to Remote Viewing*
- Former CIA remote viewing trainer; offers programs in remote viewing and related skills. Smith is the longest serving Controlled Remote Viewing teacher from the US Army's Star Gate program.

2. **Russell Targ**

- **Books:** *Do You See What I See, The Reality of ESP* (and other books)
- Remote viewing and ESP. Targ is a physicist and researcher in remote viewing and extrasensory perception (ESP).

3. **Ingo Swann**

- **Books:** *Natural ESP, Preserving the Natural Child, Psychic Sexuality* (and other books)
- A researcher of the exceptional powers of the human mind and a leading figure in governmental and scientific projects to investigate and identify the scope of subtle human perceptions.

4. **Dr. Dean Radin**

- **Books:** *Real Magic, The Conscious Universe* (and other books)
- Explores psychic phenomena from a scientific lens.

5. **ICU Academy**

- ICU Academy provides training in remote viewing and psychic abilities.

6. **Mark Komissarov and Mihaela Istrati**

- Teaches InfoVision, a method for developing and utilising extrasensory perception.

7. **The Monroe Institute**

- The Monroe Institute provides programs focused on consciousness exploration through cutting-edge audio technology and immersive retreats.

8. **The Institute of Noetic Sciences**

> • Using science to explain phenomena not previously understood and harness the best of the mind to enhance human experience.

9. **The Parapsychological Association**

> • A professional organisation of scientists and scholars engaged in the study of 'psi' (or 'psychic') experiences, such as telepathy, clairvoyance, remote viewing, psychokinesis, psychic healing, and precognition.

10. **Dr. Fritz-Albert Popp**

> • Dr. Popp's research focuses on biophysics, particularly in biophotonics.

11. **Dan Winter**

> • Winter researches the physics of mystical experiences, gravitational energy, emotions, the evolution of consciousness, sacred geometry, quantum physics, and biofeedback.

12. **Dr. Fred Alan Wolf**

> • Wolf, a physicist and author, extensively explores the connections between quantum physics and consciousness.

13. **Dr. John Hagelin**

> • Hagelin's a quantum physicist whose research focuses on the role of consciousness in the universe and the potential of meditation to influence physical reality.

14. **Bruce Lipton**

> • **Books:** *The Biology of Belief, The Honeymoon Effect, Spontaneous Evolution*
>
> • Lipton, a cellular biologist and author, explores the connections between consciousness and biology, particularly in the science of epigenetics.

15. **Gregg Braden**

> • **Books:** *The God Code, The Divine Matrix, The Spontaneous Healing of Belief* (and other books)
>
> • Braden, a scientist and author, explores the science of consciousness and the impact of human emotion on physical reality.

Soul Matters, Past Lives, Dreams, Reincarnation, and Near Death Experiences:

1. Harold Klemp

- **Books:** *The Art of Spiritual Dreaming, ECK Wisdom on Karma and Reincarnation, Past Lives, Dreams, and Soul Travel* (and other books)

- Eckankar teaches techniques to explore one's inner worlds, including past lives, dreams, and Soul Travel.

2. Dr. Michael Newton

- **Book:** *Journey of Souls* (and other books)

- Explores the experiences of souls between lives. Through deep hypnosis sessions, Dr. Newton discovered that individuals could recall their existence as eternal spirits and describe their activities in the spirit world.

3. Dannion Brinkley

- **Books:** *10 Things to Know Before You Go, Saved by the Light* (and other books)

- Brinkley shares insights gained from his near-death experiences, providing wisdom on life and the afterlife.

4. Brian L. Weiss

- **Books:** *Through Time Into Healing, Same Soul, Many Bodies* (and other books)

- Weiss explores past lives and healing through regression therapy, emphasising the impact of past experiences on the present.

5. Raymond A. Moody Jr.

- **Books:** *The Light Beyond, Life After Life: The Investigation of a Phenomenon - Survival of Bodily Death* (and other books)

- Moody explores near-death experiences, shedding light on the transformative and spiritual aspects of these encounters.

6. NDE Stories

- A web compendium of near death experiences and resources from around the world. www.nderf.org

Parthenogenesis and the Divine Feminine:

1. Marguerite Mary Rigoglioso

- **Books:** *The Mystery Tradition of Miraculous Conception* (and other books)

- Rigoglios's courses and books explore the concept of miraculous conception, particularly in the context of the divine feminine lineage.

2. Sri Sai Kaleshwara Swami

- **Books:** *The Holy Womb; The Secrets of the Divine Mother's Creation* (and other books)

- Sri Sai Kaleshwara Swami dives into the sacredness of the feminine.

3. Den Poitras

- **Book: Parthenogenesis:** *Women's Long-Lost Ability to Self-Conceive*

- Poitras explores the concept of parthenogenesis, the ability to self-conceive.

4. Jessie E. Ayani

- **Books:** *The Lineage of the Codes of Light, The Priestess and Magus Trilogy* (and other books)

- Ayani explores the codes of light within the feminine lineage, emphasising spiritual and transformative aspects, to awaken the gifts within ourselves.

5. Maureen Walton

- **Book:** *The Good Darkness*

- Walton's work reveals a hidden female creation technology called the "Blood Masteries" that activate a woman's magnetic toroidal systems. This can help a woman elevate to a superconscious level.

6. Kaia Ra

- **Book:** *The Sophia Code*

- Ra's book and programs are a divine feminine, modern sacred text. It is considered a living transmission that aims to activate spiritual evolution and awakening, reminding us of how precious we are.

7. **Margaret Starbird**

> • **Book:** *The Woman with the Alabaster Jar*

> • Starbird explores the figure of Mary Magdalene and the symbolism of the Holy Grail in relation to the divine feminine.

8. **Tom Kenyon and Judi Sion**

> • **Book:** *Magdalen Manuscript*

> • Kenyon and Sion delve into the alchemies of Horus and the sex magic of Isis, exploring sacred feminine mysteries.

9. **Elizabeth Seraphine**

> • **Program:** *The Priestess Path Lineages of Light Mystery School*

> • Seraphine offers resources and teachings on the priestess path and the divine feminine, supporting women to embody their priestess mantle and express their true power.

10. **The Lemurian Sisterhood and Shamanic Teaching Wheel**

> • **Program:** The Lemurian Sisterhood and Shamanic Teaching Wheel explores concepts related to the divine feminine.

11. **Seven Sisters Mystery School**

> • The Seven Sisters Mystery School offers teachings and practices related to the mysteries of the divine feminine that help restore the ancient way of the Priestess.

12. **Alison A. Armstrong**

> • **Books:** *The Queen's Code* (and other books)

> • Armstrong's books and programs explore the biological reasons behind the behaviour of women and help decode them.

13. **RC Blakes Jr.**

> • **Books:** *Queenology*, (and other books)

> • **Website:** Offers insights for reigning as a queen in spite of the odds, for reclaiming self-esteem, and having the courage to step into your true power.

The Alpha Male and Divine Masculine:

1. **Alison A. Armstrong**

- **Books:** *The Amazing Development of Men* (and other books)
- Armstrong's books and programs explore the journey of men from knights to princes to kings, providing insights into male development.

2. **RC Blakes Jr.**

- **Books:** *Kingology: The Return of the King* (and other books)
- RC Blakes Jr. delves into Kingology, guiding men on the path of returning to their true kingly nature.

3. **Robert Moore and Douglas Gillette**

- **Books:** *King, Warrior, Magician, Lover* (and other books)
- Moore and Gillette explore the archetypes of the mature masculine, emphasising psychological development.

4. **Robert Bly**

- **Book:** *Iron John: A Book About Men*
- Bly delves into the mythopoetic men's movement, exploring the journey to mature masculinity.

5. **Brett and Kate McKay**

- **Book:** *The Art of Manliness*
- The McKay's book and magazine offer classic skills and manners for the modern man, emphasising the traditional masculine virtues of a gentleman.

6. **David Deida**

- **Book:** *The Way of the Superior Man*
- Deida's book and program addresses the complexities of sexual and spiritual evolution in today's fast-paced world.

7. **Men Without Masks**

- Men Without Masks is a program for men to explore authentic masculinity through various resources and community.

Communication Styles of Men and Women:

1. Alison A. Armstrong

- **Books:** *The Queen's Code, Making Sense of Men* (and other books)
- Armstrong explores the reasons behind the behaviour of men and women, and fundamental differences in how we think, act, and communicate.

2. RC Blakes Jr.

- **Books:** *The Father-Daughter Talk* (and other books)
- Blakes guides men and women to embrace their inherent value and power.

3. Gary Chapman

- **Book:** *The 5 Love Languages*
- Chapman's book identifies different love languages, helping individuals understand and communicate love more effectively.

4. John Gray

- **Books:** *What Your Mother Couldn't Tell You and Your Father Didn't Know, Men are From Mars and Women are From Venus* (and other books)
- Gray's books and courses offer advanced relationship skills providing practical guidance for improving communication, and understanding the differences between men and women.

5. Esther Perel

- **Books:** *Mating in Captivity*
- Perel's work explores the complexities of maintaining intimacy in long-term relationships and the role of communication in erotic intelligence.

6. Bibi Brzozka

- Brzozka focuses on female orgasmic potential and fostering deeper intimacy through effective communication.

7. Jaiya

- Jaiya's Erotic Blueprints provide a framework for empowered sexual communication, erotic ecstasy, and enhanced understanding between partners.

Taoism and Inner Alchemy:

1. **Lao-Tzu**

- **Book:** *Tao Te Ching*

- A classical Chinese text and foundational work of Taoism written around 400 BC and credited to the sage Laozi. In eighty-one chapters, Lao-tzu's Tao Te Ching, or Book of the Way, provides imparts advice on balance and perspective, a serene and generous spirit, and how to work for the good with the effortless skill that comes from being in accord with the Tao—the basic principle of the universe.

2. **Daniel Reid**

- **Book:** *The Tao of Health, Sex & Longevity* (and other books)

- Reid explores Taoist principles related to health, sex, and longevity, including the connection between inner alchemy and well-being.

3. **Dr. Stephen Chang**

- **Books:** *The Tao of Sexology, The Great Tao* (and other books)

- Chang's work delves into the Taoist perspective on sexology, using sexual techniques to enhance health, and Taoism; emphasising inner alchemy and its transformative effects on body and mind.

4. **Dr. Felice Dunas**

- **Book:** *Passion Play* (and other books)

- Dunas's books and courses incorporate powerful Taoist principles to improve health, sex, and intimacy, rectifying sexual dissatisfaction.

5. **Mantak & Maneewan Chia**

- **Books:** *Healing Love through the Tao: Cultivating Male Sexual Energy, The Multi-Orgasmic Couple* (and other books)

- The Chia's books and courses focus on cultivating male and female sexual energy, sexual secrets for couples, and enhanced intimacy through Taoist practices. These include learning to separate orgasm and ejaculation and retention practices for longevity and vitality, leading to multiple orgasm potential.

6. **Mantak Chia and Douglas Abrams**

   • **Book:** *The Multi-Orgasmic Man*

   • This collaborative work provides insights into sexual secrets every man should know, rooted in Taoist principles. These include learning to separate orgasm and ejaculation and retention practices for longevity and vitality, leading to multiple orgasm potential.

7. **Bruce Frantzis**

   • **Book:** *Taoist Sexual Meditation* (and other books)

   • Frantzis explores the connection between love, energy, and spirit through Taoist sexual meditation, emphasising communication within intimate relationships.

8. **Richard Wilhelm**

   • **Book:** *The Secret of the Golden Flower: A Chinese Book of Life*

   • The translation of this classic work explores the teachings of Taoism, including inner alchemy and the transformative journey of life. The language is flowery and sounds poetic, yet within lie many pearls of wisdom.

9. **Hsi Lai**

   • **Book:** *The Sexual Teachings of the White Tigress: Secrets of the Female Taoist Masters* (and other books)

   • Lai delves into the teachings of female Taoist masters within the context of sexual and spiritual wisdom.

10. **Thomas Cleary**

   • **Book:** *The Taoist Classics, Volume 1* (and other books)

   • Cleary's translations provide access to essential Taoist texts, offering insights into inner alchemy and Taoist philosophy.

11. **John Heider**

   • **Books:** *The Tao of Leadership, The Tao of Daily Living*

   • Heider applies Taoist principles to leadership, emphasising effective communication and harmony in relationships.

12. **Eva Wong**

   • **Books:** Taoism: *An Essential Guide, Cultivating Stillness: A Taoist Manual for Transforming Body and Mind* (and other books)

   • Wong's books provide an overview of Taoism, including its principles of inner alchemy and communication.

13. **Robert Lawlor**

   • **Book:** *Earth Honoring: The New Male Sexuality* (and other books)

   • Lawlor explores sexual behaviour in ancient traditions like Tantra and Taoism, offering insights into redirecting male energy from excess to constructive paths. He details specific techniques used in sexual and spiritual training to harness creative potential and spiritual growth.

Martial Arts Philosophy:

1. **Patrick McCarthy**

   • **Book:** *The Bubishi*

   • Treasured for centuries by top martial arts masters, the Bubishi is a classic Chinese work on philosophy, strategy, medicine, and technique as they relate to the martial arts. For hundreds of years, the Bubishi was a secret text passed from master to student in China and later in Okinawa. No other classic work has had as dramatic an impact on the shaping and development of karate as the Bubishi. Karate historian and authority Patrick McCarthy spent over ten years researching and studying the Bubishi and the arts associated with it. His work includes groundbreaking research on Okinawan and Chinese history, as well as the fighting and healing traditions that developed in those countries, making it a gold mine for researchers and practitioners alike.

2. **Richard Kim**

   • **Book:** *The Classical Man* (and other books)

   • Kim's work explores martial arts philosophy, emphasising character development. This book shares the historically significant lives of real martial arts masters.

3. **Deng Ming-Dao**

   • **Book:** *Chronicles of the Tao: The Secret Life of a Taoist Master* (and other books)

• Ming-Dao's chronicles provide insights into the real life and wisdom of Taoist master, Kwan Saihung who was born into a wealthy martial arts family and became the thirteenth and last discipline of the grand master of the sacred mountain known as Huashan.

4. Chen Kaiguo, Zheng Shunchao, Thomas Cleary

• **Book:** *Opening the Dragon Gate: The Making of a Modern Taoist Wizard*

• The biography of Wang Liping, a modern Taoist wizard, is the true story of how a young boy becomes heir to a tradition of esoteric knowledge and practice through an arduous fifteen-year apprenticeship, learning the true source of health, healing, and long life.

5. Soke C. J. Rupert Juta

• **Book:** *Tao-Shukokairyu Odyssey* (and other books)

• Juta's work explores the martial arts style and philosophy of Tao-Shukokairyu, offering insights into the journey of a martial artist, focusing on mindset and critical thinking.

6. Gichin Funakoshi

• **Book:** *Karate-Do: My Way of Life*

• Funakoshi, known as the "Father of Karate-do," shares his journey from the secrecy of Okinawan self-defence to the global practice of martial arts. Funakoshi refined techniques and emphasised spirituality. Through anecdotes of his renowned teachers and personal trials, he unveils the essence of authentic karate and exemplifies principles of perseverance, self-reliance, and samurai ethos.

7. Bruce Lee

• **Book:** *The Tao of Jeet Kune Do*

• The book details the science and philosophy behind the fighting system Lee pioneered. It is the original mixed martial art known as Jeet Kune Do—"the way of the intercepting fist.

8. Miyamoto Musashi

• **Book:** *The Book of Five Rings*

• Musashi's classic work presents martial arts philosophy through the lens of strategy and the way of the samurai.

9. **Joe Hyams**

   • **Book:** *Zen in the Martial Arts*

   • Hyams reveals how the daily application of Zen principles developed his physical expertise and gave him the mental discipline to control his personal problems, and how understanding the spiritual goals in martial arts can dramatically alter the quality of your life.

10. **Forrest E. Morgan**

   • **Book:** *Living the Martial Way*

   • Morgan's book offers a step-by-step approach to applying the Japanese warrior's mindset to martial training and daily life.

11. **Sun Tzu**

   • **Book:** *The Art of War*

   • An ancient Chinese military treatise composed of 13 chapters and attributed to the military strategist Sun Tzu. It explores skills dedicated to warfare and how it applies to military strategy and tactics including psychology.

Shamanism and Psychedelic Plants:

1. **Mircea Eliade**

   • **Book:** *Shamanism: Archaic Techniques of Ecstasy* (and other books)

   • Eliade surveys the tradition of shamanism (at once magicians and medicine men and women, healers and miracle-doers, priests, mystics, and poets) through two and a half millennia of human history, illuminating the magico-religious life of societies.

2. **Michael Harner**

   • **Book:** *The Way of the Shaman* (and other books)

   • Harner's book introduces core shamanic practices and principles, shedding light on the role of shamans in different societies, what it is, where it came from, and how you can participate.

3. **Lynn Andrews**

   • **Book:** *The Medicine Woman book series* (and other books)

   • Andrews' books, programs, and mystery school offer training into modern-day shamanism and the divine feminine, offering insights into healing and wisdom.

4. **Andrew Weil**

- **Books:** *The Natural Mind, The Marriage of the Sun and Moon* (and other books)

- In The Natural Mind, Weil suggests that the desire to alter consciousness periodically is an innate, normal human drive. In The Marriage of the Sun and the Moon, he examines the integration of masculine and feminine energies, drawing inspiration from shamanic experiences.

5. **Carlos Castaneda**

- **Book:** *The Teachings of Don Juan: A Yaqui Way of Knowledge* (and other books)

- Castaneda's books recount Don Juan's apprenticeship with a Yaqui Indian shaman, exploring shamanic teachings and a new way of seeing the world.

6. **Eliot Cowan**

- **Book:** *Plant Spirit Medicine*

- Cowan's book explores the healing potential of plant spirits, connecting shamanic principles with the medicinal properties of plants.

7. **Jeremy Narby**

- **Book:** *The Cosmic Serpent: DNA and the Origins of Knowledge*

- Narby investigates the connection between shamanic knowledge and DNA, exploring the mysteries of consciousness and evolution.

Health (Wholeness) and Healing:

1. **Dr. Bradley Nelson**

- **Books:** *The Emotion Code, The Body Code*

- Nelson's books and work focuses on techniques that release trapped emotions to ease physical and emotional ailments.

2. **Dr. Ryke Geerd Hamer**

- **Book:** *Summary of the New Medicine*

- Hamer's work presents a very different approach to understanding cancer, how diseases develop, and the mind-body connection. His research led him to believe that diseases are a result of biological conflict, shock, or trauma (if not a result of poison or an injury). He discovered that each biological conflict leaves a visible mark in the brain (confirmed by a CT scan) and that the nature of the conflict predetermined the site of the disease. The result of his research was the creation of a disease chart that accurately describes the biological conflict cause of each disease, the exact location in the brain where the focus is found, and how the disease manifests during the conflict active phase and resolution phases.

3. David R. Hawkins

• **Books:** *The Spectrum of Consciousness Explained: A Proven Energy Scale to Actualize Your Ultimate Potential, Power Vs. Force, Healing and Recovery* (and other books)

• Hawkins' work explores healing and recovery from a spiritual perspective, integrating consciousness and health. He developed a map that defines a range of values, attitudes, and emotions that correspond to levels of consciousness and provides practical applications to help people heal and evolve to higher levels of consciousness and energy. He posits that an individual's power and level of consciousness can be enhanced through greater integrity, understanding, and compassion.

4. Lars Muhl

• **Book:** *The Gate of Light: Healing Practices to Connect You to Source Energy* (and other books)

• Muhl's book is an introduction to the long-forgotten healing methods of the Essenes, and offers useful tools, meditations, and visualisations for modern-day practitioners.

5. Deepak Chopra

• **Book:** *Quantum Healing: Exploring the Frontiers of Mind/Body Medicine* (and other books)

• Chopra's work combines Western medicine, neuroscience, and physics with the insights of Ayurvedic theory to show that the human body is controlled by a "network of intelligence" grounded in quantum reality. Not a superficial psychological state, this intelligence lies deep enough to change the basic patterns that design our physiology, with the potential to overcome illness.

6. Michael Breus

• **Book:** *The Power of When*

• Breus's work on the science of sleep presents a groundbreaking program for getting back in sync with your natural rhythm (chronobiology) by making minor changes to your daily routine. Working with your body's inner clock for maximum health, happiness, and productivity becomes easy and fun.

7. Felice Dunas

• **Book:** *Passion Play* (and other books)

• Dunas's books and courses focus on healing through pleasure; incorporating powerful Taoist principles to improve health, sex, and intimacy, leading to more meaningful connections and a more satisfying life.

8. Nadia Volf

• **Book:** *Mysteries of the Ear: Secrets of Well-Being*

• Volf is the creator of the Auricular Causative Diagnostic method. Her work reveals the extraordinary powers of the auricular (ear) acupuncture points, making it possible to provide relief for everyday ailments.

9. Konstantin Sukhov

• **Book:** *Clinical Hirudotherapy: Practical Guide: Book 1. General Hirudotherapy* (and other books)

• Sukhov's guide explores the therapeutic use of medicinal leeches, known as hirudotherapy, to address a wide array of health complaints.

10. HP Ekkehard Scheller

• **Book:** *Candidalism*

• Scheller's work examines the impact of candida overgrowth on health and well-being, contributing to the understanding of candidalism. Borrelias, viruses, and other pathogens have learned to camouflage themselves to keep from being attacked by our immune system and strong drugs. Thanks to Dark Field Microscopy of blood and Radionic Testing, Ekkehard Sirian Scheller discovered the camouflaged Candida fungi, which varied their shape to keep from being detected. Due to the fermentation of glucose, extreme mycotoxins are produced, which destroy the mucosal system due to constant corrosion. As a result, many secondary diseases arise.

11. Artour Rakhimov

• **Book:** *Breathing Slower and Less: The Greatest Health Discovery Ever* (Buteyko Method) (and other books)

• Rakhimov's book explores the health benefits of the buteyko breathing method and its impact on well-being. Learn how breathing retraining can prevent and alleviate many diseases, along with insights from clinical trials, lifestyle factors, and breathing retraining techniques. Embark on a journey to long-term health and vitality.

12. James Nestor

• **Book: Breath:** *The New Science of a Lost Art*

• Nestor's exploration of breath delves into the science and art of breathing, emphasising its crucial role in health.

13. Ben Greenfield

• **Book:** *Boundless: Upgrade Your Brain, Optimize Your Body, & Defy Aging*

• Greenfield is a walking encyclopedia of biohacking wisdom, blending cutting-edge science with practical tips for a vibrant life. As a health consultant, speaker, and author, he aims to optimise life for boundless energy and fulfilment through his books, podcasts and coaching. He specialises in longevity, anti-aging, biohacking, and positive psychology.

14. Dr. Gabor Maté

• **Book:** *When the Body Says No: The Cost of Hidden Stress, The Myth of Normal: Trauma, Illness, and Healing in a Toxic Culture* (and other books)

• An addiction expert, Dr. Maté is the creator of the psychotherapeutic approach, Compassionate Inquiry. His books and work explore the connection between stress, emotions, and addiction and disease, offering insights into the mind-body connection.

15. Bessel van der Kolk

• **Book:** *The Body Keeps the Score: Brain, Mind, and Body in the Healing of Trauma*

• Van der Kolk's influential work explores the impact of trauma on the body and mind, offering approaches to healing.

16. Dr. Anna Lembke

• **Book:** *Dopamine Nation: Finding Balance in the Age of Indulgence*

• Lembke's book explores the role of dopamine in modern society and its impact on health, addiction, and well-being.

17. **Jonathon Aslay**

> • **Book:** *What The Heck Is Self-Love Anyway?*

> • Aslay's book and relationship coaching focus on self-love as a fundamental aspect of health and well-being, contributing to personal development and healthy relationships.

18. **Barbara Ann Brennan**

> • **Book:** *Hands of Light: A Guide to Healing Through the Human Energy Field* (and other books)

> • Brennan's book explores energy healing through the human energy field, offering insights into holistic health practices.

19. **Emily Matweow**

> • Emily Matweow is a master energy healer and medical intuitive specialising in energy healing, medical intuition, removing blocks, and empowering clients to regain balance, clarity, and peace.

20. **Alvin De Leon**

> • Dr. Alvin De Leon focuses on empowered health through the principles of Dr. Hamer's German New Medicine, based on the 5 biological laws.

21. **Brent Bruning**

> • **Book:** *The Power in Your Hands*

> • Bruning's work specialises in breaking through trauma patterns using biological blueprints as seen in the hands, offering innovative approaches to healing. Web: www.thepowerinyourhands.com

> • **Bonus for readers! Coupon Codes for:**
>> • A 2-hour Hand Analysis + Life Pattern Session
>> Coupon code: StoryMaster (receive $100 off)
>> • The Shift or The Hero's Journey program: Mastering your shadows to break through to your exalted Self
>> Coupon code: StorymasterProduct (receive $100 off)

22. **David Sereda**

> • David Sereda offers frequency-based healing products and programs, exploring the intersection of sound, vibrational alignment, and health.

23. **Medical Medium Anthony William**

• **Books:** *Brain Saver, Thyroid Healing, Medical Medium* (and other books)

• Medical Medium Anthony William was born with the unique ability to converse with the Spirit of Compassion, who provides him with extraordinarily advanced healing information far ahead of its time. He is considered a chronic illness expert and is the originator of the global celery juice movement and Brain Shot Therapy.

24. **Vibrational Revelations with Elena Bensenoff and Alejandro Ferradas**

• Using integrative and quantum medicine, paired with vibrational frequency measurements of your level of consciousness (based on the work of David R. Hawkins's map of consciousness), Elena Bensenoff and Alejandro Ferradas offer resources on vibrational healing and frequency readings for clients.

25. **Bio-resonance Life Flow: Health Scans & Consultations with Yvette Farkas**

• Get a clear picture of your health with a bio-resonance scan. It tests for viruses, bacteria, mold, parasites, allergies, food intolerances, heavy metals, inflammation, and more. Even the strength of the auric field is shown. Detailed health scans provide insights into energetic imbalances and blocks to health, empowering you to make more informed decisions to increase vitality, wellbeing, and energy. Web: www.bioresonancescans.com

26. **Thich Nhat Hanh: International Plum Village Community**

• Thich Nhat Hanh is a Zen master, the founder of Plum Village, numerous movements and charities, and the author of over 100 books focusing on mindfulness.

27. **HeartMath Institute**

• The HeartMath Institute explores the connection between heart health, emotions, and overall well-being, offering practical tools for self-regulation.

28. **Bryan Johnson**

• Bryan Johnson's biohacking protocol focuses on health optimization, contributing to personalised approaches to wellbeing.

29. **Edgar Cayce's Association for Research and Enlightenment (A.R.E.)**

• **Book:** *The Essential Edgar Cayce* (and other books)

• The Association for Research and Enlightenment (A.R.E.) offers body-mind-spirit resources and educational programs that foster personal transformation through the wisdom embedded in the extensive collection of Edgar Cayce's readings. Edgar Cayce is a twentieth-century seer and intuitive healer. The book features Cayce's most intriguing and influential readings, and a biographical introduction to his life.

30. Diagnostic Testing of One's Biological Age

• TruDiagnostic offers diagnostic testing of one's biological age, providing insights into overall health and longevity.

Yoga Philosophy:

1. Swami Sivananda

• **Books:** *Bliss Divine, Practice of Bhakti Yoga* (and other books)

• Swami Sivananda is the founder of the The Divine Life Society, the inspiration behind the Sivananda Yoga Vedanta Centres and Yasodhara ashrams, and the author of over 300 books.

2. Swami Sivananda Radha

• **Books:** *Mantras; Words of Power, Radha; Diary of a Woman's Search* (and other books)

• Swami Sivananda Radha is the founder of Canada's first ashram - Yasodhara Ashram, and opened the Yoga Vedanta bookstore.

3. Swami Vishnu-Devananda

• **Books:** *Meditation and Mantras, The Classical Illustrated Book of Yoga* (and other books)

• Swami Vishnu-Devananda founded the Sivananda Yoga Vedanta Centres and is the author of numerous books.

4. Swami Satchidananda

• **Books:** *The Yoga Sutras of Patanjali, Key to Peace* (and other books)

• Swami Satchidananda founded Integral Yoga International and Satchidananda Ashram - Yogaville and is the author of numerous books.

5. Swami Satyananda

- **Books:** *Asana, Pranayama, Mudra, and Bandha, Yoga Nidra* (and other books)
- Swami Satyananda founded International Yoga Fellowship Movement and The Bihar School of Yoga, and authored numerous books.

6. The Bhagavad Gita

- The Bhagavad Gita (Sanskrit: "Song of God") is a foundational text in yoga philosophy, offering profound teachings on duty, righteousness, and the path to spiritual realisation.

7. Sri Kaleshwar

- **Book:** *The Holy Womb - The Secrets of The Divine Mother's Creation: A Rendering of the Teachings of Sri Sai Kaleshwara Swami* (and other books)
- Kaleshwar's work delves into the mysteries of divine consciousness, contributing to the understanding of spirituality and self-realisation.

8. Yogacharya B.K.S.Iyengar

- **Book:** *Light on Yoga: The Bible of Modern Yoga* (and other books)
- B.K.S.Iyengar founded the Ramamani Iyengar Memorial Yoga Institute (RIMYI) and authored numerous books.

9. TKV Desikachar

- **Book:** *The Heart of Yoga: Developing a Personal Practice* (and other books)
- TKV Desikachar developed Viniyoga and founded the Krishnamacharya Yoga Mandiram (KYM), and has authored numerous books.

10. Sri Aurobindo + The Mother

- Sri Aurobindo is the author of several books and co-founder with The Mother of the Sri Aurobindo Ashram. In addition to spending 50 years overseeing the growth of this many-faceted spiritual community, The Mother established Sri Aurobindo International Centre of Education, and an international township called Auroville.

Ayurveda (The Science of Life):

1. **Dr. Robert E. Svoboda**

   • **Books:** *Ayurveda: Life, Health and Longevity, Prakriti: Your Ayurvedic Constitution* (and other books)

   • Dr. Robert Svoboda's books and programs provide a comprehensive overview of Ayurveda, exploring its principles and practices for maintaining health and longevity.

2. **Dr. Vasant Dattatray Lad**

   • **Books:** *Ayurveda: The Science of Self-Healing: A Practical Guide, The Complete Book of Ayurvedic Home Remedies* (and other books)

   • Dr. Vasant Lad is the founder of the Ayurvedic Institute and the author of 12 books. His work disseminates the timeless principles and practices of Ayurvedic - The Science of Life.

3. **Dr. David Frawley and Dr. Vasant Dattatray Lad**

   • **Book:** *The Yoga of Herbs: An Ayurvedic Guide to Herbal Medicine*

   • This collaborative work explores the intersection of Ayurveda and herbal medicine, offering insights into natural healing.

4. **Dr. David Frawley**

   • **Book:** *Ayurveda and the Mind: The Healing of Consciousness* (and other books)

   • Dr. David Frawley is the founder of The American Institute of Vedic Studies and author of several books exploring the rich knowledge of Ayurveda.

5. **Maya Bri. Tiwari**

   • **Book:** *Ayurveda: Secrets of Healing* (and other books)

   • Maya Tiwari is the founder of The Wise Earth School of Ayurveda and Mother Om Mission (MOM). Her books and work share the healing path of Ayurveda, unveiling its secrets for healing and maintaining balance.

6. **Amadea Morningstar**

   • **Book:** *The Ayurvedic Cookbook* (and other books)

   • Amadea Morningstar is the founder of the Ayurveda Polarity Therapy and Yoga Institute. She is an author, speaker, and Ayurvedic practitioner and instructor.

Sacred Geometry and Physics:

1. Gyorgy Doczi

- **Book:** *The Power of Limits: Proportional Harmonies in Nature, Art, and Architecture*

- Doczi explores the concept of proportional harmonies in various aspects of life, art, and architecture through sacred geometry.

2. Robert Lawlor

- **Book:** *Sacred Geometry: Philosophy and Practice* (and other books)

- Lawlor's work delves into the philosophical and practical aspects of sacred geometry, exploring its significance in diverse disciplines.

3. Matila Ghyka

- **Book:** *The Geometry of Art and Life*

- Ghyka's book connects geometry with art and life, revealing the inherent mathematical principles that underlie both.

4. Les Brown

- **Book:** *The Pyramid*

- This resource explores the use of pyramids for healing and meditation, offering insights into their potential benefits.

5. NOAA - Magnetic Field Calculators

- The NOAA website provides tools for calculating the Earth's magnetic field, including declination, useful for aligning pyramids with the Earth's magnetic forces.

6. David Sereda

- Sereda, a researcher and filmmaker, offers insights into UFOs, quantum physics, and spirituality, providing a deeper understanding of the universe and human potential.

7. David Wilcock

- Wilcock, a researcher and lecturer, explores the convergence of science and spirituality, investigating topics like UFOs, consciousness, and the universe's mysteries, often incorporating sacred geometry and metaphysical concepts.

Finances and Wealth:

1. Ken Honda

• **Book:** *Happy Money: The Japanese Art of Making Peace with Your Money*

(and other books)

• Ken Honda explores the relationship between happiness and money, offering insights from Japanese philosophy to create a harmonious connection with finances.

2. T. Harv Eker

• **Book:** *Secrets of the Millionaire Mind: Mastering the Inner Game of Wealth*

• Eker delves into the mindset and psychological aspects that contribute to financial success, providing guidance on cultivating a wealthy mindset.

3. Robert G. Allen

• **Book:** *Multiple Streams of Income: How to Generate a Lifetime of Unlimited Wealth!*

• Allen introduces the concept of creating multiple income streams for long-term financial success, outlining strategies for generating wealth.

4. Sam Rossi and Andra Pickens

• **Book:** *Quantum Networking: How to Play the Game that the Wealthiest and Happiest People Play... Starting Today*

• Rossi and Pickens explore the principles of quantum networking, offering a unique perspective on building connections for financial success.

5. George S. Clason

• **Book:** *The Richest Man in Babylon*

• Clason's classic imparts timeless financial wisdom through parables set in ancient Babylon, addressing principles of wealth-building.

6. Thomas J. Stanley and William D. Danko

• **Book:** *The Millionaire Next Door: The Surprising Secrets of America's Wealthy*

• Stanley and Danko reveal common traits and habits of self-made millionaires, challenging stereotypes and offering practical insights for building wealth.

7. **Napoleon Hill**

- **Book:** *Think and Grow Rich*

- Hill's seminal work outlines principles for success and wealth, emphasising the power of mindset and goal-setting.

8. **Morgan Housel**

- **Book:** *The Psychology of Money: Timeless Lessons on Wealth, Greed, and Happiness*

- Housel explores the psychological aspects of money management, providing insights into the behaviours that influence financial decisions.

9. **Alex Hormozi**

- **Book:** *$100M Offers: How to Make Offers So Good People Feel Stupid Saying No*

- Hormozi shares strategies for crafting irresistible offers that create compelling opportunities for financial success.

10. **Tony Robbins**

- **Book:** *MONEY Master the Game: 7 Simple Steps to Financial Freedom* (and other books)

- Robbins' work provides practical steps for achieving financial and personal freedom to live your best life.

11. **Robert & Kim Kiyosaki**

- **Book:** *Rich Dad, Poor Dad: What the Rich Teach Their Kids About Money - That the Poor and Middle Class Do Not!* (and other books)

- The Kiyosaki's books, programs and games offer educational programs for financial freedom that are simple enough for a 9-year old to understand.

12. **Bob Proctor**

- **Book:** *You Were Born Rich*

- Proctor's teachings focus on unlocking one's innate potential for wealth and success, emphasising the abundance within each individual.

13. **Ramit Sethi**

- **Book:** *I Will Teach You to Be Rich*

- Sethi's book and courses provide practical advice on personal finance, covering topics such as saving, investing, and creating a rich life.

Behaviour and Body Language:

1. Chris Voss

- **Book:** *Never Split the Difference: Negotiating As If Your Life Depended On It*
- Voss, a former FBI negotiator, shares negotiation techniques and strategies, providing insights into effective communication and persuasion.

2. Vanessa Van Edwards

- **Book: Captivate:** *The Science of Succeeding with People*
- Van Edwards explores the science of interpersonal communication, offering practical tips and strategies for connecting with others.

3. Joe Navarro

- **Book:** *What Every Body is Saying*
- Navarro, a former FBI agent, decodes nonverbal communication, providing insights into reading body language for improved understanding and communication.

4. Rebecca Zung

- **Book:** *How to Negotiate with a Bully (Narcissist)*
- Zung provides guidance on negotiating with challenging personalities, particularly narcissists, offering strategies for effective communication.

5. Ramani Durvasula, PhD

- **Book:** *It's Not You*
- Dr. Durvasula explores relationships with narcissists, providing insights into understanding and navigating these challenging dynamics.

Transmitted and Channelled Information:

1. Kryon

- **Books:** *Don't Think Like a Human, The Twelve Layers of DNA, The Indigo Children, The Women of Lemuria* (and other books)
- Kryon offers channelled information via books, programs, and retreats, providing spiritual insights and teachings, contributing to personal and collective transformation.

2. **Abraham Hicks**

> • **Books:** *Ask and It is Given: Learning to Manifest Your Desires, The Astonishing Power of Emotions* (and other books)
>
> • Abraham Hicks, channelled by Esther Hicks, shares teachings on the law of attraction, manifestation, and spiritual guidance via books, programs, and retreats.

3. **Law of One**

> • The Law of One provides channelled material offering perspectives on spirituality, the nature of reality, and the evolution of consciousness.

4. **Ashayana Deane**

> • **Books:** *Voyagers: The Sleeping Abductees - Volume 1, Voyagers: The Secrets of Amenti - Volume 2* (and other books)
>
> • Ashayana Deane's work explores ascension mechanics and multidimensional consciousness, providing insights into spiritual evolution.

5. **Sarah Landon**

> • **Books:** *The Wisdom of the Council: Channelled Messages for Living Your Purpose, The Dream, The Journey, Eternity, And God: Channeled Answers to Life's Deepest Questions*
>
> • Sarah Landon shares channelled information and spiritual teachings to assist individuals on their path of self-discovery and personal growth.

6. **Emily Matweow**

> • **Book:** *INTUITION: Discover 11 Different Kinds* (and other books)
>
> • Emily Matweow is a master energy healer and medical intuitive, providing insights and guidance for holistic well-being.

7. **Lee Harris**

> • **Book:** *Conversations with the Z's*
>
> • Harris is an energy intuitive, author, and musician. His grounded, practical teachings focus on the expansion of awareness to help you live a more heart-centred life.

Conscious Leadership, Mentorship, and Coaching:

1. **MindValley**

    • MindValley offers personal development and education programs, focusing on holistic growth, consciousness, and well-being.

2. **Regan Hillyer**

    • Regan Hillyer provides coaching and mentorship for individuals seeking personal and financial transformation, emphasising conscious leadership.

3. **Juan Pa Barahona**

    • Juan Pa Barahona offers coaching and mentorship, guiding individuals towards personal and professional success through conscious leadership.

4. **Marcel Szenessy**

    • Marcel Szenessy provides seminars and coaching, emphasising personal development and conscious leadership for individuals and organisations.

5. **Yvette Farkas**

    • Yvette Farkas is a health-based coach and mentor, an author, and practitioner of ancient healing practices taking people back to their health and their hearts.

6. **Daria Vodopianova**

    • Daria Vodopianova contributes to conscious leadership and mentorship, focusing on empowering individuals in their personal and professional journeys.

7. **Tony Robbins**

    • Tony Robbins is a renowned life coach and motivational speaker, offering programs and events focused on personal development, wealth creation, and leadership.

8. **Brent Bruning**

    • Brent Bruning's work specialises in breaking through trauma patterns using biological blueprints as seen in the hands, offering innovative approaches to healing through in-depth coaching and mentorship.

Other:

1. David Wilcock

- **Book:** *Awakening in the Dream:Contact with the Divine* (and other books)
- Wilcock explores topics related to consciousness, spirituality, and the nature of reality, providing insights into awakening and self-discovery.

2. Jessie Ayani

- **Book:** *The Brotherhood of the Magi* (and other books)
- Ayani's work explores mystical and esoteric themes, offering insights into ancient wisdom and the spiritual journey of the Magi.

3. Vladimir Nikolaevich Megre

- **Book: Anastasia:** *Ringing Cedars of Russia* (9 books)
- Megre's "Anastasia" series revolves around a Siberian recluse named Anastasia, sharing her wisdom on nature, spirituality, and the interconnectedness of all life.

4. Michael A. Singer

- **Book:** *The Surrender Experiment: My Journey into Life's Perfection* (and other books)
- Singer recounts his personal journey of surrendering to life's flow, providing a profound exploration of spiritual surrender and personal growth.

5. Zecharia Sitchin

- **Book:** *The Anunnaki Chronicles: A Zecharia Sitchin Reader* (and other books)
- Sitchin's collection delves into ancient Sumerian texts, offering interpretations and insights into the possible extraterrestrial influence on human history.

6. Peter Ragnar

- **Book:** *Finding Heart: How to Live with Courage in a Confusing World*
- Ragnar shares his perspective on courage and navigating life's challenges, providing insights and practical wisdom for personal development.

7. Richard P. Feynman

- **Book:** *Surely You're Joking, Mr. Feynman! Adventures of a Curious Character*

• Feynman's memoir offers humorous anecdotes and reflections on his life as a physicist, showcasing his curious and playful approach to understanding the world.

8. Joseph Campbell

• **Book:** *The Power of Myth* (and other books)

• Campbell explores the power of myth and its role in human culture, drawing connections between ancient stories and contemporary life.

9. Dan Millman

• **Book:** *Way of the Peaceful Warrior*

• Millman's novel combines fiction and autobiographical elements, conveying spiritual teachings through the story of a young athlete's journey toward enlightenment.

10. Rudolf Steiner

• **Book:** *Bees*

• Steiner delves into the spiritual significance of bees and their role in the natural world, offering insights into the interconnectedness of life.

11. Jacqueline Freeman

• **Book:** *Song of Increase: Returning to Our Sacred Relationship with Honeybees*

• Freeman explores the sacred relationship between humans and honeybees, emphasising the spiritual and ecological importance of these creatures.

12. Richard Bach

• **Book:** *Illusions: The Adventures of a Reluctant Messiah* (and other books)

• Bach's philosophical novel explores the nature of reality, illusion, and the potential for each individual to discover their divine nature.

13. Hermann Hesse

• **Book:** *Siddhartha*

• Hesse's novel follows the journey of Siddhartha, exploring themes of self-discovery, enlightenment, and the spiritual path.

14. **Robin Sharma**

   • **Book:** *The Monk Who Sold His Ferrari*

   • Sharma's book combines fiction and self-help, telling the story of a successful lawyer's spiritual journey toward a more meaningful and fulfilling life.

15. **Neale Donald Walsch**

   • **Books:** *Conversations With God: An Uncommon Dialogue (Books 1-3)* (and other books)

   • Walsch's book presents a dialogue with the divine, offering profound insights into spirituality and the soul's journey.

Devices for Health and Healing:

1. **David Sereda's Products (the largest frequency library in the world)**

   • Sereda offers a diverse range of products, including frequency libraries, designed to promote health and well-being through vibrational and energy principles. Web: www.davidsereda.co

2. **Safe Laser**

   • A new generation of lasers for therapeutic use. The Safe Laser family has analgesic and anti-inflammatory effects and speeds up healing and regeneration of the body. Web: www.safelaser.hu/en

3. **Jonathan Goldman's Chakra Chants Tuning Forks**

   • Goldman's tuning forks are designed to align with chakras, offering a sound-based approach to balancing and harmonising energy centres in the body

4. **Bio-Well**

   • Bio-Well is a device that measures and visualises the human energy field, providing insights into overall wellbeing and energy balance. Web: www.bio-well.store

5. **SomaVedic**

   • Products that utilise frequency therapy and natural science to harmonise spaces and water, and reduce the impact of harmful EMFs. Web: www.somavedic.com

The Most Important Things I Learned From This Book: